What Love Looks Like

USA TODAY BESTSELLING AUTHOR

NIKKI ASH

All life decisions should be made
with the sun rising and the
waves crashing.

Dedication

To all the fighters in the Fight Club who allow me to keep writing my single parent and secret baby books... this one's for you.

One

Sawyer

"TO SAWYER!" LISA LIFTS HER GLASS, AND I HOLD MY BREATH IN fear of whatever she's about to say, praying nobody can hear her over the loud hotel bar music. "May you use your new position to educate the minds of our future generation, help shape our troubled youth, and never get arrested for sleeping with a student."

Raising my glass, I clink it with hers, groaning at her crassness but not bothering to reprimand her. Over the years, I've learned she says whatever she wants, and calling her out will only make her worse.

Besides, her toast isn't entirely off base since I've just accepted my first teaching position, all thanks to a teacher who *did* sleep with her student and was fired—something I will definitely not be doing.

"To me," I agree because, despite her drunken toast, I'm proud of myself. I've busted my ass these past four years, and now I have a degree in English education to show for it. After this summer, I'll be stepping into a classroom and doing what I love: teaching. I've dreamed of this for so long, it felt like just that... a dream. But I worked hard and made it happen, and now my dream is a reality.

"Scott's calling me," Lisa says, eyeing her phone. "He must be here. I'm going to go find him." She swallows down the last of her drink and then kisses my cheek before taking off to chase down her husband.

"Congratulations," a masculine voice says, making me twist to the side to face him. When I meet his eyes, they're dancing with mirth, and I know he heard everything Lisa just said. "A teacher, I assume?"

I nod, taking a sip of my drink. "Yes, twelfth grade English, and thank you."

His eyes scan my body, just long enough to take me in but not for so long that he looks like a perv. "I think you have a better chance of sleeping with your student than shaping their minds." My eyes go wide, not expecting that. "Have you seen those TikTok videos?" He cringes, his entire body dramatically shuddering. "I'm not sure any of them are capable of being shaped or educated. But if you were my English teacher in high school, I have no doubt I would've tried to hit on you."

I take a moment to check him out. Underneath the white Nike hat he's wearing low on his forehead is a hint of brown hair that appears to be shaved short. The tiny age lines around his brown eyes tell me he's older and has lived life—probably in his early, maybe mid-thirties. If I had to guess, he's about a foot taller than my five-foot-four self and, based on the way his biceps fill out his white polo shirt, he works out on the regular.

"So..." he prompts, making me look back up at him.

"What?"

"If I were your student, would you sleep with me?" he asks, his crooked smile making him look significantly younger.

I choke out a laugh and throw the rest of my drink back. "No. No man is worth the amount of work I've put into getting this degree."

His smile softens, and he nods in understanding. "I'm Hudson Matthews."

"Sawyer Addison."

"It's nice to meet you, Sawyer Addison." He leans in close, so only I can hear whatever it is he's about to say, and I catch a whiff of his masculine scent. It's crisp with a tad of smokiness and a hint of vanilla. "This is the part where I should insert some clever pickup line, but I'm years out of my youth and rusty on the flirting, so how about I just offer to buy you a drink? And if you say yes, I'll ask you to dance in a little while so I can show you my moves."

A sexy grin spreads across his face, and I find myself laughing in appreciation at his straightforwardness. I don't get out often, but when I do, he's right—guys my age always have the corniest pickup lines. Women respect a man more when he simply lays it all out instead of wasting our time playing games.

"You can definitely buy my drink, and after a few, if I still like you, I'll consider dancing with you. But I have to warn you, dancing is rather personal, right up there with sex, so you're going to have to make quite the impression on me in order to get me out onto that dance floor."

He chuckles darkly. "Challenge accepted."

"I'm drinking Jack and Coke." I push my empty glass his way.

"Ah, a woman after my own heart." He raises his glass, and the bartender rushes over.

"What can I get you, Mr. Matthews? Another drink?"

"Yes, please, and one for the lady."

"Yes, sir." The bartender goes about making the drinks, and I glance at him curiously.

"What?" he asks, tilting his head to the side slightly.

"He knows your last name. Are you a regular?"

Though it's my first time at this resort on Hilton Head Island, the extravagance of this place doesn't seem like somewhere you would come to grab a drink after work. Maybe he's vacationing here as well and has spent a lot of time at the bar. If that's the case, he's probably not someone I should be talking to. The last thing I need is to spend my time with another alcoholic.

"No." He shakes his head. "I started a tab earlier, so he probably read my name on my credit card."

I sigh in relief, then chastise myself for jumping to conclusions. Not every man has a problem with alcohol.

The bartender delivers our drinks, and Hudson raises his glass. "To Sawyer," he says with a devilish twinkle in his eye. "May you mold the youth and not sleep with them while doing so."

I smack his arm and glance around, making sure no one is paying attention. "Not funny!" I hiss through my laughter, lifting my drink and taking a sip.

"C'mon... It's a little funny."

Rolling my eyes, I take another sip and side-eye him. "Keep it up, and we won't make it to that dance floor."

With a playful smirk, he raises his hands in mock surrender. "All right, all right, I'll behave. So tell me, what brings you to the island?"

"A graduation present from my sister."

"Nice. Is she the woman who ran out a few minutes ago?"

"That'd be her. Her husband has no sense of direction.

She came here with me for the weekend to hang out and do a little sister bonding. He's picking her up so they can fly out tomorrow morning for their anniversary trip. I'm sure she's walking around the hotel trying to explain to him how to find the bar."

Hudson laughs, and the carefree sound has me smiling.

"What brings you here?" I ask.

"Vacation," he says simply. "I have some life decisions to make, and what better place to think about them than at a killer resort on the beach? All life decisions should be made with the sun rising and the waves crashing."

"It's my first time at the beach," I admit sheepishly.

"Really?" His eyes widen in surprise.

"Yep. I grew up on a farm in Tennessee, which is obviously nowhere near the ocean. My parents are homebodies and perfectly content to simply work on the farm. I always dreamed of going to the beach, of sinking my toes into the soft sand and swimming in the ocean, maybe swimming with some dolphins." I shrug. "But once I graduated from high school, life happened, and it took me a little longer than I hoped to actually get to the beach."

Hudson smiles. "Well, you're here now. Is it everything you dreamed of?"

"Maybe," I mutter, downing my drink.

"What do you mean, maybe?" He quirks a brow, silently imploring me to explain.

"I haven't actually been in the water yet," I confess.

"But you said you've been here for a couple of days."

"I know, and we've seen the beach. We just haven't been in the water yet."

"What are you waiting for?"

"I don't know. We've been hanging out at the pool. I'm going to go...eventually."

"Let's go now."

"What?" I shriek, shaking my head. "No way."

Hudson's brows hit his forehead. "You're scared."

"No," I splutter. "I'm going to go. I'm here until Saturday. But it'll be in the daylight...not when it's dark out. There can be sharks or jellyfish in the water. The tidal waves could drown us. We can get sea lice."

"You're totally fucking scared." He grins like a Cheshire cat.

"I am not." I glare. "I've just been enjoying the pool and cabanas. Besides—"

"Found him!" Lisa says, cutting me off as she pulls her husband up to the bar and blocks my view of Hudson. "You got another drink and didn't get me one?" She pouts.

"Actually, Hudson got it for me."

"Who?" she asks, confused.

"That would be me," Hudson says, turning the attention on him.

"Oh, shit," Scott gasps. "You're Hudson Matthews."

"Who?" my sister and I both ask.

Scott shakes his head. "The QB?"

"The what?" I ask, still having no idea what language he's speaking.

Hudson stands and reaches out for my hand, and when I eye it, not giving him mine, he laughs. "Don't worry, I'm not going to drag you into the ocean. I just want to dance with you." He shoots me a sexy wink, and even though I want to argue that he hasn't earned that dance, I give in and place my hand in his.

With a cocky smirk, he guides me onto the dance floor. I

glance back at my sister, who's staring at us in shock, while Scott whispers something into her ear. When I look back at Hudson, he pulls me into his arms as "Anyone" by Justin Bieber comes on.

Our bodies sway to the music, and with each passing song, Hudson proves he does, in fact, have moves. Our eyes stay locked on each other as if everything around us has faded away, and we're the only two people here.

When a slower, sexier song comes on, he pulls me closer until my body is flush against his. He slides his hands down my hips to my backside, landing on my ass, and tugs me closer. I can see it in his eyes that he's going to kiss me... \and I'm totally going to let him.

And then my phone buzzes in the back pocket of my jeans, reminding me of my obligations. "I have to go," I tell him. "I'm sorry but thank you for the drinks and the dance."

I step back, breaking our sizzling chemistry, and he opens his mouth, probably to ask why—and I'd like to think also to ask me to stay—when Lisa appears at my side.

"Give us a moment," she says to Hudson as she pulls me to the side.

"Hol-y shit, girl." She fans her face dramatically and then presses the back of her hand against my forehead.

"What the heck are you doing?" I ask with a confused laugh.

"I was checking to see if you have a fever. You guys were so hot on the dance floor. I can't believe you haven't caught fire."

"Oh my God, stop. I have to go g—"

"No, you don't. I have it handled. Stay here and enjoy your night."

"But—"

"Nope, everything will be fine. Now go." She pushes me back toward where Hudson is waiting for me. "You're twenty-four years old, sis. Now go act like it!"

I want to argue with her—tell her that being twenty-four means responsibility and obligations, not staying out late with a sexy man I've only just met—but she's right. I've been busting my ass for the past four years in school, and I've not only graduated but also secured a job. I deserve a night out.

"You sure?" I ask her, feeling like I need to give her an out.

"Yes! Now stop worrying and go have fun. We'll either see you later tonight or tomorrow morning, but if it's tomorrow morning, make sure you let me know so I don't worry." Then she saunters off, leaving me standing here wondering what the hell I'm doing.

"Everything okay?" Hudson asks over the loud music.

"Yeah. I, um, actually don't have to leave after all."

A smile splits across his face. "Yeah? Does that mean you're all mine tonight?"

The thought of being *his*, even if only for a few hours, has butterflies exploding in my belly.

"I'm all yours."

"Let's go." He entwines our fingers and wastes no time hauling me off the dance floor. I try to ask him where we're going, unsure if he misunderstood and plans to take me back to his place and have his way with me—and then I wonder if I'd actually mind. I've never had a one-night stand before, but if I'm going to have one, it might as well be with someone who, based on the way he dances, has some moves in the bedroom.

Once we're outside, the scent of the ocean breeze hits my

senses hard, and I take a second to breathe in the fresh air. Even though it's still warm outside, it feels cooler out here because the number of gyrating bodies in the bar made it hotter inside. With a few Jack and Cokes running through me, I'm a bit tipsy—the good kind, where you feel light and carefree, and your inhibitions are taking a walk, but you haven't drunk enough that you dread waking up tomorrow with a hangover.

When we turn the corner, Hudson stops in front of one of the expensive-looking golf carts I've only seen the staff driving and bows dramatically. "Your chariot awaits, my lady."

I find myself giggling at his silliness as I slide onto the passenger seat. He sprints around the front and jumps in, turning a key and stepping on the gas like he's a part of *The Fast and the Furious* golf cart edition.

"Are we going to get arrested for stealing a golf cart?" I yell over the wind whirring around us as he recklessly drives down the sidewalk, taking the corners as if he's in a real race. I should be concerned about us flipping or hitting someone, but as he laughs at my question, only picking up his speed in response, I find myself laughing along with him. I can't remember the last time I felt this carefree. I'll have to thank Lisa later for affording me this time to, as she put it, act my age.

We take the winding path in several directions, and since the resort is beyond massive, I have no idea which way we're heading. Hudson's driving as though he's on a mission, so I hope he knows. When he finally stops, I look in front of us and see where he's taken us.

"Oh, no!" I'm about to dart out of the golf cart and run in the opposite direction, but before I can, Hudson whisks me over his shoulder like I'm a feather and jogs down the sand straight toward the Atlantic Ocean.

"Hudson!" I scream, banging on his backside and praying he isn't about to do what I think he's going to do. When he cackles like a damn psycho and pulls my heels off my feet, I close my eyes, preparing for the worst. Only the worst doesn't come, and when I open my eyes, he's dragging me down his front slowly until my bare feet are sinking in the sand and our bodies are flush.

"We're here," he says softly, jutting his chin out. Turning

around, I come face-to-face with the dark water. Hudson snakes his arms around my waist and rests his chin on my shoulder as he walks us forward until the waves lap at my toes and then my entire feet. I'm wearing jeans, so the material around my ankles gets wet, but I ignore it as I take deep breaths of the salty air. My heart instantly calms, mesmerized by the way the water meets the sky, and the moon shines down enough to light up the softly rolling waves.

After staring out at the water for a few beats, Hudson guides us back enough to sit in the sand without getting soaked. He drops down first and then spreads his thighs so I can sit between his legs. For several minutes, we sit in silence, watching as the waves roll in, stop at our feet, then roll back out. I barely know this man, and I should probably be concerned about being alone with him on the beach, away from the safety of the resort, but all I can feel is comfortable. From the moment our eyes locked, I felt an instant connection to him.

"So what do you think?" he finally asks, breaking the silence.

"It's beautiful," I breathe, sighing against his chest.

"Thank you."

"Once the sun is up and we're in proper attire, we'll have to go in the water so you can get the full experience."

I laugh softly and nod even though I know that won't be happening. While tonight has been fun, I won't be seeing Hudson again. For some crazy reason, that thought has my chest feeling heavy as if I'm already missing Hudson and this moment before it's even over.

I'd like to blame what I do next on the alcohol, but we already know I'm not drunk, so really, I have no excuse, though it's something I've thought about doing since the moment Hudson spoke to me.

Turning in place, I straddle Hudson's lap. I lift his hat off his head and spin it around so the bill faces backward. And then, before I can second-guess my crazy behavior, my mouth connects with his.

Two

Sawyer

AS MY LIPS CURL AROUND HIS AND MY TONGUE SWEEPS INTO HIS mouth, I briefly note that Hudson's lips are soft yet firm. He tastes sweet with a hint of spice from the Jack and Coke he was drinking mixed with something I can't quite pinpoint. I expect the kiss to be quick, and I'm preparing to pull back and apologize for attacking him when he grips the globes of my ass and stands, carrying me through the sand. A few seconds later, my back hits a soft surface, and I open my eyes long enough to see I'm on a double lounge chair under Hudson in a cabana.

With his arms caging me in, and his warm body pressing against mine, he deepens the kiss, his tongue swirling around mine. When his knee parts my legs, and his thigh rubs against my center, I groan into his mouth, arching my back in need.

He pulls back slightly, his heated gaze meeting mine. "Fuck, you taste so damn good." His lips brush against mine softly, and then his tongue glides across the seam of my lips. Our mouths connect once again, and my arms tighten around his neck to pull him closer. We stay like this, devouring each other with our mouths and grinding against each other through our clothes, but neither of us takes it any further. My head is screaming, *abort! You're acting crazy and reckless*, but my body is shoving my head to the side and covering her mouth, saying, *get it, girl. You do you and worry about the fallout later.*

"I can't remember the last time I made out with someone," Hudson murmurs when he breaks the kiss. "I feel like I'm a horny teenager all over again."

He smiles against my mouth, and I laugh in response. "I don't remember it being as good when I was a teenager," I admit, pressing a chaste kiss to his lips.

He snags my bottom lip with his teeth and nibbles on my flesh before releasing it. "No, it definitely wasn't."

He rolls off me, taking me with him, so we're lying on our sides, facing each other. His legs are trapping my own, and his arms are around me. And even though we're no longer kissing, I somehow feel as though our bodies are just as connected.

"Tell me something about you," he says.

"Like what?"

"Anything. I don't care. I want to know everything."

My stomach tightens at his admission, remembering it's late, and our time is limited. "I've wanted to be a teacher since I was seven," I blurt out, unsure why I chose that piece of information. "I would get leftover worksheets from my teacher to bring home and make my sister and brother do them so I could grade them. It drove them nuts, but I was the youngest, the *oops baby* born years after them, so they spoiled me and would do them."

"And now you're a teacher." He tucks a wayward hair behind my ear, and a shiver rushes through my body.

"I am." A proud smile spreads across my face. "Well, at

least I will be in August when school officially starts."

"You're going to kill it," he says with such conviction, I have no choice but to believe him.

"Okay, your turn. Tell me something about you." His mouth twists up in thought, and I remember something from earlier. "Wait. How does my brother-in-law know you? Or know your name? And what the heck is a QB?"

"Three questions? You only gave me one thing," he says with a chuckle, but something about it is different than the carefree laughter he's been giving me, and it makes me nervous.

When he doesn't answer me, I start to pull back, needing to distance myself from him. "If you don't want to tell me, you don't have to..."

Before I can slip away, he grips my hips and tugs me toward him. "It's not that..." He takes a deep breath, and I wait for him to finish his sentence, but when he doesn't, I've had enough.

"Look, it's been fun, and you don't owe me anything, but I don't do secrets." I peel his hands off me and scramble off the lounger, but Hudson grabs me again, pulling me back down and into his arms.

"It's not a secret," he rushes out before I can push him away. "Honestly, I was shocked you didn't know who I was."

"A bit full of yourself?" I scoff. "How would I know who you are?"

He chuckles softly, shaking his head. "I take it you don't watch football?"

"Umm, no. What does that have to do with...?" And then it hits me. QB. I might not watch football, but I've been around my dad, brother, and brother-in-law enough during football season to know what it stands for. I just wasn't thinking about it at the time. "You're a quarterback."

"That I am. For the New York Bluebirds."

"Can you throw good?"

"I'm all right." He shrugs, but the sexy smirk on his face tells me he's more than good.

"Have you ever won a Super Bowl?"

He laughs. "Yeah, a few times."

"How many?"

"I have five rings."

I have no clue if that's considered a lot or not, but I

decide to mess with him anyway. "That's it?" I scoff playfully, which makes his smile widen. "This other football player I once dated had six."

"I call bullshit," he growls, rolling me onto my back and hovering over me. "Only one other player has more than me."

"Maybe I dated him." I shrug, holding back my laughter.

"How old are you?"

"Twenty-four."

"He's twice your age. Didn't happen."

"I'm out with you, and you're twice my age," I goad.

"I'm only thirty-six." He glares playfully.

"Practically an old man."

"I'll show you an old man." Sitting up, he straddles my thighs, and his fingers go straight to my sides, tickling the hell out of me and making me snort out the most unladylike laugh.

"Oh my God! Stop it!" I wheeze out, trying to no avail to push him away.

"Take it back," he demands, continuing to tickle me.

"Fine! You're not an old man. Now stop!" I beg through my laughter.

Thankfully, he listens. "Damn right." He rolls back over and takes me with him, encircling his arms around me. "But seriously, I wasn't trying to keep it a secret. I was just shocked you didn't know who I was."

"So, what, you assumed because you're like this decent football player who can throw a ball, everyone *must* know who you are? Sounds kind of egotistical to me." I roll my eyes dramatically, making him laugh.

"When you're on hundreds of commercials and billboards for various endorsements like Nike and Gatorade, it tends to happen. Once I realized you didn't know who I was, I kind of enjoyed the fact that I was just a guy sitting at a bar flirting with a woman."

"That was your flirting?" I joke, scrunching up my nose in mock confusion.

"Don't make me tickle you again," he warns.

"What are you doing so far from New York?"

"Vacation. Preseason doesn't start for a couple of months. My parents used to bring us here...Well, to the island, not the resort...when we were little, so it seemed like the perfect place to escape and relax."

"What are you trying to escape from?"

"Life." He laughs, but it sounds kind of sad.

We're both quiet for a few minutes, during which time Hudson rolls onto his back and guides my head to his chest and my leg over his, entwining our bodies. I go with it, relaxing against him and enjoying the tranquility of the light breeze as the ocean waves lap at the beach.

"Tell me something about you," he says after a few minutes, getting back to our original little game of getting to know each other.

"I have a rule against dating anyone famous."

He laughs, but when I don't join in, he lifts slightly, forcing me up as well, so he can look me in the eyes. "Wait, are you serious?"

"Yeah, but we're not dating, so we're good."

He clears his throat and nods once, then lies back again.

"Tell me something," I say through a yawn, the craziness of the night creeping up on me and hitting me hard. My head goes back to his chest, and my eyelids flutter closed. I try to pry them open, determined to stay awake, but I'm so tired. I tell myself I'll rest them for a few minutes while we lie here and talk. It's not as if we can fall asleep out here.

"I'm unemployed."

This time, it's my turn to snort out a laugh. "If that's your funny attempt to prove you're not famous so I'll date you, it's not going to happen."

He chuckles under his breath, the vibration rattling me. "I'm actually not joking," he says, running the tips of his fingers through my hair and down my back. I release a deep, relaxed breath as I continue to fight sleep. "My contract was up this season, and I have to sign a new one. I actually should've already signed it. It's a good deal. Better than what most QBs my age are offered."

"So, why haven't you?" I ask, barely awake.

"That's a damn good question."

BUZZ. BUZZ. BUZZ. BUZZ.

The feeling of my phone going off in my back pocket has me groaning and stretching, not wanting to get out of bed but knowing I have to.

My arm hits something hard, and a masculine voice hisses, "Ow, shit!" putting me on alert because...why the hell is there a man in bed with me?

My eyes pop open, the sunlight nearly blinding me just as my phone goes off again. I fly up, taking in my surroundings as the events from last night come back to me.

"Morning," Hudson says, his voice sounding way too throaty and sexy.

Buzz. Buzz. Buzz. Buzz.

"I think someone's trying to get ahold of you."

"Huh?" I ask, momentarily in a haze over the fact I just spent the night on the beach—literally—with a man I've only known for thirty seconds.

"Your phone." He scrubs his hand over his face, and the movement causes his shirt to drag up, exposing his dark happy trail. "It's going off."

My phone... "Shit!" I pull it out of my pocket and find several missed calls and texts from Lisa.

Where are you?

You never came back?

WTF Sawyer!

If you don't answer soon, I'm calling the police.

Seriously? You better be dead to not be answering me.

That's it! I'm calling 911.

The last text was sent less than a minute ago. I jump off the lounger and quickly hit my sister's name to call her before she seriously calls the police.

"Where the hell are you?" she screeches over the phone as I haul ass up the beach toward the hotel. "I asked you to let me know if you were staying out."

"I'm sorry!" I huff, practically out of breath from sprinting through the sand. "I didn't mean to. We were talking, and I must've fallen asleep. I'm on my way to the room now."

Lisa sighs in relief. "I'm just relieved you're okay. I mean, I figured you were safe since you're with Hudson fucking Matthew, but I'm sure even five-time Super-Bowl-winning football players are capable of murder. Remember that one guy? What was his name?"

"Lisa!" I bark, speed walking down the sidewalk. The woman has a knack for getting off topic. She can start discussing brownies and end with talking about an orgy. "You know who Hudson is?"

"I didn't at first, but Scott told me. That's the only reason I let you go off with him. He's way too well-known to kidnap and rape a woman."

"Thanks for the heads-up, sis."

"What?" she asks innocently as if she doesn't know my damn rule about not dating anyone famous. Granted, I never thought in a million years I would ever meet someone else who's famous, but still...

"Never mind." I stomp into the elevator and press the number to our floor. "I'll be there in two minutes."

I get up to the room, and using my mobile app, I unlock the door. Scott is sitting on the couch eating room service while my sister shoves her clothes into a suitcase.

"Where's Abby?" I ask, looking around for my little girl.

"Dropped her off at camp. When she asked where you were, I told her you were having a sleepover with a special friend." She winks, and I shoot her a glare.

"What time is it?" I glance at my phone and see it's only half past eight.

"Time for us to head out," Scott says, wiping his mouth and standing. "Our flight leaves at eleven." He puts his arm around me. "But before I go...please tell me you got me an autograph."

"A what?" I slide out from under his arm.

"An autograph. C'mon, Sawyer, you seriously didn't get one? I texted you to get one," he whines.

"No, you didn't." Lisa playfully shoves him.

"What?" He shrugs. "The guy is the best QB in the league, and your sister spent the night with him while I was on babysitting duty."

"I highly doubt my sister had time to ask him for his autograph while she was with him. Unless he totally sucked in bed." Lisa glances at me. "Did he suck in bed?"

"I didn't sleep with him. We were lying on the beachside loungers, talking, and fell asleep. That's it."

"Lame. Did he ask for your number at least?"

"No." I roll my eyes. "We..." Oh, shit! "I left him."

"What?"

"I woke up all foggy, forgetting where we were, and then I called you, scared you were going to call the police, and I left him. Like I actually hightailed it up to the room and didn't even say goodbye to him."

Lisa shakes her head. "Only you."

"I'm assuming that means you didn't get my autograph." Scott pouts like a damn kid.

Lisa glares at him and pops the handle up on the suitcase.

"I can't believe you're leaving." I pull my sister into my arms.

"I know," she says, hugging me back. "It was so much fun having a girls' weekend. I miss you, sis. We need to do it again soon."

"I miss you more." I kiss her cheek.

"You'll be back for Abby's birthday, right?"

"Of course," she says, pulling back. "Enjoy yourself this week. Relax, have a few drinks, go swimming in the damn ocean..."

"I will," I promise. "Thank you." I glance at Scott. "Both of you. This place, this trip...it's too much, but I really appreciate it, and I know Abby does too."

"You don't have to thank us," Lisa says. "You're my baby sister, and you only graduate from college once."

"But if you want to thank us, you could get me that autograph," Scott adds with humor in his voice.

"It's highly unlikely I'll be seeing him again."

"Why not?" Lisa asks. "He's staying here too, isn't he?"

"Yeah, but he's on vacation. I doubt a famous football player wants to spend his time with a single mom and her four-year-old daughter."

"Hey," Lisa chides. "He would be damn lucky to spend his time with you and my niece, but even so, that's why I made sure the resort has a kid's camp. So you can have some adult time while Abby has fun playing with kids her own age. You deserve a little R and R."

"Yeah, yeah." I hug her one more time. "Have fun in the rainforest."

"Oh, we will." Scott grabs the suitcase from Lisa. "Oh, hey, while you were talking, did you by any chance find out if he's signing with the Bluebirds for next season?"

"Scott!" Lisa shoves him forward.

"What? Everyone's been on pins and needles waiting to

know. It's all ESPN's talking about. Maybe he told her."

"All he told me was that he's unemployed."

Scott's eyes go wide in horror. "Oh, shit. That can't be a good sign. Listen, if you see him again, maybe give him some of that motherly advice you always give to Abby like don't give up...blah, blah, blah. If he doesn't play this year, the team's going to suck."

Lisa rolls her eyes and drags him out the door. "Bye, Sawyer. Love you!"

"Love you more!" I call back.

Since Abby will be at the kid's exploration camp for the next few hours, I take a quick shower to rinse the night off and then throw on a bikini so I can go lay out by the pool.

On the first day we arrived, my sister surprised her with going to the camp. I felt guilty about pawning her off on other people, so I went to pick her up after a couple of hours to spend some time with her. Only she got upset, saying she made the best of friends, and begged me to let her stay.

The next day, she woke up, got dressed, and practically dragged me to the kids camp. After that, I stopped feeling guilty. If she wants to spend the week having a blast with other kids, then more power to her. I'll happily lie out by the pool and drink overpriced mudslides courtesy of my brother, who sent me way too much spending money for this trip.

After grabbing a coffee and a pastry from the on-site Starbucks, I find a shaded lounge chair and plop down, ready to enjoy my morning. I have my earbuds to listen to music, my e-reader so I can read my latest romance novel, and my laptop, in case I want to work on some lesson plans.

I'm sipping my drink—and pretending not to look for Hudson—when my phone rings. I check to see who it is, and when I see it's the kids camp—I put their number and info into my phone in case of an emergency since Abby is too young for a cell phone—I quickly answer it.

"Hello."

"Good morning, Ms. Addison. This is Jody calling from the Kids Exploration Camp."

"Yes, is everything okay?"

"There's been a little incident..."

"Is my daughter okay?" I ask, shooting up and grabbing my stuff, already on my way to my little girl.

"Yes, she's okay, but there's been a minor altercation, and

we're going to need you to come and get her. We're at the main room. We'll explain once you get here."

"Okay, I'm on my way."

I hang up and sprint the entire way there. Once I'm at the door, I scan my phone to let me in. One of the things I love about this place is how secure everything is to ensure the kids are safe and well cared for.

I nod at the woman at the front desk, and she smiles tightly at me, making me nervous. "Abby is right through that door," she explains, knowing which kid is mine.

I'm barely to the door when I hear a voice I'm fairly certain sounds familiar. "You need to say you're sorry." And then another, younger voice. "I'm not saying sorry. He had it coming!"

What the heck is going on?

I barge into the room and freeze when the bright blue eyes, belonging to the voice I knew I recognized from last night, meet mine.

"What are you doing here?" I ask him, my gaze darting from him to my daughter, who's in tears.

"Mommy!" Abby sobs, running over and wrapping her

tiny arms around me. I lift her into my arms even though she's too big to be held, and she latches onto me, nuzzling her face into my neck.

"Someone tell me what's going on," I demand. "Why is my daughter crying?" I look at Hudson in confusion. "What are you doing here?" I ask him again.

"That kid pushed Abby," says the little boy standing next to Hudson, pointing a finger at another little boy, who is on the opposite side of the room.

"She was taking too long!" the little boy sneers.

"Oh well!" says a little girl, who I didn't notice before. "She can take a hundred hours if she wants to. Right, Lucas?"

"Yeah," agrees the boy, whose name must be Lucas. "She can take a hundred years."

"Lucas, Presley," Hudson growls. "Enough. Lucas, say it..."

"That's not fair, Dad!" Lucas says, glaring at Hudson. "You told me if anyone ever hurts my sister, I can punch him because it's not cool to hurt a girl. Abby isn't my sister, but she's a girl, and she's my friend. He pushed her and made her cry, so I punched him, and I'm not sorry." Lucas crosses his arms over his chest and turns his glare to the boy who apparently pushed my daughter. And then it hits me...He called Hudson "Dad."

"That's your son?" I blurt out.

"Yep," Hudson says. "And his sidekick in crime"—he pulls the little girl closer—"is my daughter, Presley."

My mouth falls open in shock. Holy shit. The sexy, rich, amazing kisser, famous football player Hudson Matthews is a dad. Well, shit, I didn't see that one coming.

Three

Hudson

SHE'S A MOM. THE WOMAN WHO HAS BEEN IN ALMOST EVERY thought since last night is a mom. When she ran away this morning, I wanted to hunt her down, but I needed to get back to my room so I could take the kids to camp. I had planned to look for her once they were situated, but not even an hour later, I got a call to come down and get my kids because Lucas had punched a kid in the face as my daughter stood by his side, cheering him on. And by the sound of it, he did it to protect Sawyer's daughter from a bully.

"Excuse me, I'm looking for my son," says a woman with

fake blond hair and a faker tan, her voice coming out nasally. "Oh, Maximillian, there you are." She runs over to the bully and envelops him in her arms, her strong perfume damn near choking me to death.

"What's going on here?" she demands, turning to face everyone.

"It seems Max pu—" the camp manager begins, but the woman cuts her off.

"It's Maximillian," she corrects.

"I'm sorry, it seems your son pushed Abby off the playground equipment, and as a result, another child punched him."

"What?" she shrieks, steam billowing from her ears. "Who punched my son?"

"I did," Lucas speaks up, jutting his chin out like the little badass he is. "Max is a bully and pushed Abby, making her cry."

The woman glares daggers at my kid, and I step in front of him, needing to take control of the situation before she can say something she'll regret.

"Lucas was taught it's never okay to hurt a girl, and if he

sees one hurt, to defend her. He shouldn't have punched your son, though, and I'll be speaking to him."

"And you think it's okay for your son to put his hands on mine?"

"No, I don't," I tell her. "And I'll be speaking to him."

"Good."

"Just like I hope you'll be speaking to your son about laying his hands on a girl."

She scoffs and looks at her son. "Did you push that girl?"

"I was just trying to help her go," her son says, playing the innocent card. "I didn't mean to hurt her."

"There you go," she says, lifting her nose into the air. I've dealt with enough of these entitled, stuck-up moms over the past several years to know better than to argue with them. They know no wrong, and they're the reason their children will grow up to be entitled assholes, just like their parents.

"That's not true!" Presley yells. "Max pushed her off, and when she fell and cried, he laughed and told her she was a baby."

"Look," the camp manager says with a sigh. "There are a lot of stories, but what it boils down to is that we can't have anyone hurting anyone, regardless of the reasoning. I'm going to ask the parents of everyone involved to take their kids with them today to give them time to cool off, and tomorrow, we'll start fresh. But if this happens again, the child who put his or her hands on another child will not be allowed back."

"This is ridiculous!" the bully's mom hisses. "I have plans at the spa today, and my husband is on the golf course. What am I supposed to do with him?"

I refrain from saying what I want to say, like *how about you take care of your damn kid?* and grab my two before either of them says anything else to make it worse.

But before we can make it out, the stuck-up witch steps in front of me. "This is all your little brat's fault. Now I—"

"Excuse me," Sawyer says, cutting in. "Don't you dare call a child a brat. That sweet, protective little boy was standing up for a young girl, and if more boys were like him, we would have fewer women being abused. He was taught to respect women, and maybe if your son was taught the same, we wouldn't be here right now." She turns toward Lucas, giving the woman her back, and kneels in front of him. "Thank you for protecting my little girl. Maybe in the future, unless you're in a situation where hitting someone is necessary, instead, you can tell an adult. That way, you're not using violence to stop violence, and you don't risk getting in trouble, but you're still making sure she's okay. What do you think?"

The way she speaks to my son with respect and patience reminds me of his mother, and my heart swells in my chest, the way it always does whenever I think about her.

"Yeah," Lucas says, looking at Max. "I'm sorry for punching you, but if you ever hurt Abby or my sister, I'll make you—"

"And now it's time to go," I say, cutting him off. "Thank you for saying sorry." I glance at the camp manager, who's clearly forcing herself not to laugh at my son. "I'll have a more thorough conversation with my kids, and when they return tomorrow, they'll behave."

"Well, we won't be returning," the stuck-up bitch announces. "I'll not only be reporting this to the hotel, but I'll be taking my business elsewhere." Dragging her son behind her, she stomps out of the room.

"Good riddance," the camp manager says under her

breath, her eyes going wide when she realizes she spoke loud enough for us all to hear. "Umm, I'll see you guys tomorrow."

"Can we go swimming and get ice cream?" Presley asks once we're outside.

"Yeah!" Lucas agrees. "And then go to the beach!"

"And can Abby come?" Presley adds.

"Yeah! Abby, you want to get ice cream and go swimming?" Lucas asks as though no parents are a part of this plan.

"Can we, Mommy?" she asks Sawyer softly, her cute puppy dog eyes matching her mom's green ones.

"Oh, umm…" Sawyer glances at me, unsure what to say. "Let me talk to Hudson for a moment." She finds a table and sets her daughter in the chair. "You guys wait right here."

The kids do as she says, and then she guides me a few feet away, just out of hearing distance. "I didn't mean to run away this morning…" she begins, but I shake my head.

"I get it. You had to get back to your daughter."

"I didn't know you were a dad…"

"And I didn't know you were a mom." I glance at our kids, who are talking and laughing as they play some hand slap game. "Last night was about us. Being a single dad, I rarely get those nights, so it was nice to just be me, and I thoroughly enjoyed spending time with you."

Sawyer's cheeks blush a gorgeous shade of pink. "I enjoyed our time together too."

"Dad, have you decided?" Presley asks, her lack of patience coming out.

"What do you say?" I ask Sawyer. "Nothing says good job for punching a bully like ice cream and swimming."

Sawyer barks out a laugh. "You sure? I don't want to intrude…"

"You're definitely not intruding. And from what I've seen, both of my children are quite taken with your daughter. Seems we have a thing for the Addison women." I wink playfully, and she snorts.

"Okay, ice cream and swimming…in the pool."

"And the beach," I add, walking away before she can argue.

"So, can we?" Lucas asks, hopeful.

"You think you deserve to have ice cream and go swimming after getting kicked out of camp?" I ask him, wondering what he'll say.

"Um, well..." He shifts in his seat.

"The truth."

"He hurt Abby and made her cry. Maybe I shouldn't have hit him, but he's really mean."

"I get that," I say, sitting next to him. "But Abby's mom was right. Next time, you need to let an adult handle it. Using violence to stop violence isn't the right answer."

"What about when I'm an adult?" he asks, curious as always.

"There are times when violence is needed, but it should never be the first answer. Understand?"

"Yeah, I guess." He shrugs, clearly not sorry for punching that little shit, and I don't blame him. I would've done the same thing. I've taught my son to protect women, and he did what he was taught.

"So, does that mean we can get ice cream?" Presley asks. "I really, really want mint chip."

"Me too! I want mint chip!" Abby agrees, her eyes lighting up in excitement, looking like a mini version of her mom.

"I thought cookie dough was your favorite," Sawyer says to her daughter. "Have you ever had mint chip?"

"Well, no..." Abby says softly, "but it's Presley's favorite, so it's mine too. She's my best friend."

Sawyer bites on the corner of her bottom lip to stifle her laughter. "Okay, then."

"Ice cream?" Lucas asks again to get us back on track.

"Hmm, I don't know. What do you think, Sawyer?" I ask. "Do these guys deserve it?"

"I think so. But maybe only one scoop instead of two since they got kicked out of camp." She winks at the kids, and they all cheer in excitement, jumping out of their chairs and heading in the direction of the ice cream shop.

"No running!" she yells after them.

"BEACH!" PRESLEY YELLS, ICE CREAM COVERING HER MOUTH, cheeks, and the front of her cover-up. I swear more food ends up on her than in her belly.

"Yeah," Lucas agrees. "Let's go to the beach instead of the pool. I want to use my boogie board. Pleassseee."

I glance at Abby, waiting for her to join in, but she stays

quiet, just like her mom, and both of them look slightly uncomfortable. And that's when I remember what Sawyer told me last night—that they've never actually been in the ocean.

"Why don't we go to the pool?" I say to my kids. "The one with the pirate ship and waterslide."

"Daaadd," they both whine. "We want to go to the beach."

"I want to play with my sandcastle buckets," Presley says.

"You guys go," Sawyer says to me. "Thank you for the ice cream." She looks at Lucas. "And for coming to Abby's defense."

"Why don't you guys come?" Lucas asks. "I can let you use my boogie board if you promise to be careful."

Sawyer smiles softly at his generosity while Abby chews on her bottom lip, looking torn. It's clear she wants to join my kids, but she's scared.

"That's very nice of you," Sawyer says, "but we're going to go hang out at the pool."

Both my kids pout but already respect her enough not to argue.

"Will you be at camp tomorrow?" Abby asks, hopeful.

She hasn't talked much, at least not while we've been eating our ice cream, but it's clear my kids adore her. They seem to do about ninety percent of the talking, and she adds in when she feels it's necessary.

"Yeah, we'll be there," Lucas answers. "It's a beach day."

Abby's eyes go wide in fear, looking right at her mom.

"We can spend the morning at the splash pad," Sawyer says to her daughter. "And then afterward, you can go hang out."

"The splash pad?" Lucas asks in disgust, and before I can stop him, already knowing what's going to come out of his mouth, he finishes his thought. "That's for babies!"

Abby's eyes well up with tears, and she turns away from everyone. "I want to go home," she says to Sawyer. "Please."

"Of course." Sawyer glances at all of us and smiles sadly. "Thank you again for everything."

She and her daughter turn to walk away, but Presley runs toward her before they go. "Wait, don't you want to go to the beach with us? I'll share my buckets with you."

"Pres..." I start, unsure of how the hell to handle this. I'm not an expert with kids. Really, I'm only good with my own, and that's only because they're little badasses, thanks to my half-ass parenting. Don't get me wrong, I love my kids to death, but that doesn't mean I know what the hell I'm doing.

Abby shakes her head, trying to get away so nobody will see her upset, but Presley is a lot like me—stubborn and determined as fuck. "Abby, wait." She turns her shoulder, forcing a teary-eyed Abby to look at her. "Why are you crying?" she asks, her voice filled with confusion and sadness.

Sawyer meets my gaze, silently begging me to get my kids away so her daughter won't be embarrassed, but before I can speak up, Abby answers her. "I can't swim in the ocean."

"But you swim in the pool," Presley says. "You swim like a fast fish."

Abby giggles through her tears. "I can't swim in the ocean, though. I've never been." She steps toward Presley and whispers, "I'm scared."

"Well, that's stupid," Lucas says. "It's the same thing, and my dad is the best swimmer ever. So if you drown, he'll save you."

Abby's eyes bug out. "I don't wanna drown. I'll die."

"Only if my dad doesn't save you, but he will. Right, Dad?

You'll save her if she drowns."

Sawyer looks like she's going to throw up, and Abby glances at me like my answer will determine the course her life will take. I should probably stop this conversation, but really, Sawyer is being ridiculous. They're here at the beach, and they'll be safe. And if they never go in, they'll always be afraid.

"Yeah," I tell her, kneeling in front of her. "If you want to swim in the ocean, I'll make sure you don't drown. Would you like to go swimming in the ocean?"

A smile spreads across her tiny face, and she nods slowly. "Mommy and I want to swim with the dolphins, like a real fish."

"I want to, too!" Presley agrees. "Can we, Dad?"

I stand back up, chuckling. "How about we start with just swimming in the ocean, and we can work our way up to chilling with the dolphins?" My eyes meet Sawyer's. "What do you say? Want to give the ocean a try? I promise not to let either of you drown."

I shoot her a playful wink, and she groans. "You're lucky our kids can hear us, or I would have a few choice words for you.”

I bark out a laugh. “C’mon, fishes.” I throw my arm around Sawyer. “Let’s go swimming.”

Four

Sawyer

I CAN'T BELIEVE I SOMEHOW GOT COERCED INTO GOING INTO the ocean by Hudson and his cute, crazy children. One minute, I was lying under the stars with the man discussing his professional future, and the next, I'm standing in the camp office, finding out he not only has two children, but my daughter has apparently taken quite a liking to both of them—something almost unheard of. Since she was a baby, she's always been on the quieter, shy side. It takes a lot to get her to talk and react, but I've learned over the years that nothing is wrong with her. She's just picky with who she gives her time to. So for her to be so attached to Hudson's kids so quickly tells me she feels they're good people.

I figured we would get ice cream and then go our separate ways, but somehow that turned into Abby and me standing in front of the ocean.

"Mommy, look at the waves!" Abby squeals in excitement. Now that she knows she's safe, she's practically buzzing to finally get into the water. It boggles my mind how quickly she trusted Hudson when he promised not to let her drown.

"I'm gonna ride them all," Lucas says with his board in his hand as his dad sprays sunscreen all over his face.

"You're going to stay close to the shoreline," Hudson corrects.

"But Dad..."

"No buts. Along the edge unless I'm out there with you."

"I'm not going in," Presley says. "I'm building a castle with a moat."

"What's a moat?" Abby asks.

"A big river that keeps everyone away. Daddy says if the camera people don't leave us alone, he's going to build a house with a moat."

I laugh at that as my eyes meet Hudson's. I didn't plan to spend the day with my non-one-night stand, and I have to admit, just because the sun came up didn't mean the chemistry between us faded. Every time he looks at me, I swear he wants to eat me alive. Or maybe I'm just thinking that because I totally want him to devour me.

"Presley, we're all going to go in once so Abby and Sawyer can go in, then you can build your castle," Hudson tells his daughter.

"Okay," she agrees easily, dropping her sand toys and whipping her bathing suit cover off. "C'mon, Abby." She takes my daughter's hand and guides her toward the water, and I pull out my phone to take a million pictures of her first time in the ocean.

"You too," Hudson says, taking my hand and mimicking his daughter's actions with a playful smirk. "Don't worry," he whispers, so nobody can hear. "I'll keep you safe." Butterflies flutter in my belly, and I have to tamp them down.

"Wait, I need to take my cover up off," I tell him, letting go of his hand and removing the material to expose my bikini. His eyes scan down my body, drinking me in like he's dehydrated and I'm his only source of water, and I have to admit, I love how thirsty he is. After I had my daughter, I went through a lot of shit with her father and lost a part of myself. I put on some weight and wasn't happy with my body. After we cut ties, I worked hard to lose the weight and become the person I wanted to be—mentally and physically—and I finally feel like I'm there.

"Can you put sunscreen on me too?" I ask Hudson, turning around and giving him my back, knowing full well what I'm doing.

I hear a faint growl, and then the liquid is being sprayed onto my shoulders. "Make sure it's even," I toss out, glancing back at him.

His eyes burn into mine as he drops the bottle, and his hands land on me, rubbing the sunscreen in. The way he massages my flesh has me wanting to lie down and beg him to give me a full-body massage, but then I remember where we are and who we're with. I step away and clear my throat. "Thank you."

"My turn," he says, lifting his shirt over his head. My jaw damn near hits the sand as I take in his hard chest and six-pack. It's clear he takes care of his body, which makes sense because of his profession.

"Do all football players look like you?" I blurt out, seriously regretting not paying attention to the sport.

His eyes narrow into slits, and he steps closer to me. "It doesn't matter because the only man you're looking at is me."

"For now," I sass. "When does football season start again?" I tap my chin thoughtfully, and his heated glare darkens just before he scoops me up over his shoulder and slaps my ass.

"I think someone needs to be cooled off," he growls, heading straight for the water while I shriek and beg him to put me down. "Girls, Lucas, stay right there for a minute."

I glance back at the kids and notice our daughters are both laughing at Hudson's antics while Lucas shakes his head with a smile on his face. Hudson runs into the water and then lowers me, submerging us both underneath and leaving only our faces safe from the salt water. Instinctually, my legs wrap around his muscular waist, and his hands grip my ass to hold me up. The cool and refreshing water feels good against my warm skin.

"That wasn't so bad, was it?" he asks, reaching out and

tucking several strands of hair behind my ear.

"What are we doing?" I murmur. Our faces are so close that with just a simple movement from either of us, we'd be kissing.

"Right now? We're taking our kids swimming. But later, my hope is to finish what we started last night because I'd really like to explore every inch of your body." He moves my body up and down a couple of times, so my center rubs against his hard body, forcing a low groan out of me.

"Hudson..."

"I know," he says, dropping me so we're no longer touching. "Later..."

I'm about to argue, but he's already grabbing my hand and guiding us back out of the water toward the kids.

"All right. Who's ready to go in the water?"

All three kids cheer. Lucas grabs his board and runs toward the water while Presley takes Hudson's hand. Abby glances at Hudson, and he extends his other hand out for her. I'm shocked when she takes it and smiles up at him, making it clear she trusts him completely.

"C'mon, Mommy!" Abby says to me. "We're gonna swim

with the dolphins."

Hudson chuckles. "I'm not sure we'll see any dolphins right now, but they're definitely out there somewhere."

We spend the next several minutes playing in the shallow water. Abby loves it, asking if she can bring some water and sand back with us to show her grandparents, and of course, Presley offers her one of her buckets to do so.

When the girls have had enough, I offer to take them back to play in the sand while Hudson stays out with Lucas so he can play on his board. We spend the day on the beach. Hudson rented a huge cabana that comes complete with couches, lounge chairs, and even a flat-screen TV in the corner. A little while later, I learn it also comes with a waitress, who makes sure we stay hydrated and brings us lunch.

"Today has been fun, thank you," I tell Hudson as we carry our exhausted daughters up the sidewalk with Lucas and his board following. It's early afternoon, and since the kids are beached out, we decided to call it a day.

"I'm glad we could be a part of your first official time at the beach," he says.

"You've spoiled us, and my daughter will be shocked tomorrow when she learns going to the beach doesn't equal a mini-house and a waitress." I wink playfully, making him laugh.

"Daddy, can Abby come over and watch a movie with me?" Presley asks, half-asleep. Abby is already passed out in my arms for her afternoon nap. I thought naps would end once she started school, but she gets so worn out from learning all day that she'll take a small power nap when she gets home. In a couple of hours, she'll be reenergized and ready to go again.

"If it's okay with Sawyer, I don't see why not." He glances at me with heat in his eyes. "What do you say? Dinner and a movie?" He waggles his brows, so only I can see, and my insides tighten in response.

I should be responsible and say no. We've only just met, and we're already spending a lot of time together. We should probably take some time apart. But there's just something about him that has me gravitating toward him. I shouldn't already trust him, but I do. I've watched him closely all day with our kids. He's patient and kind and playful. He's a damn good hands-on dad from what I've seen, and I'm not ready to end our time together yet.

"Dinner and a movie sounds great."

After exchanging numbers to communicate, we part ways since he's staying in a different building. I take Abby back to our room for her nap, and while she's sleeping, I shower and get dressed. While I'm hanging up our wet suits, a text message comes through from Hudson.

Hudson: All day I couldn't stop thinking about you.

I suck in a sharp breath at his admission. I'd be lying if I said I wasn't thinking about him too. We might've been together all day, but with three kids, the world revolves around them, putting whatever was brewing between us on the backburner.

Me: What were you thinking about?

Hudson: I don't like how things ended between us last night.

Me: How did things end?

Hudson: That's the problem...the night ended. I want

a to be continued.

I get what he's saying. The chemistry was clearly there. But I don't know what he wants, knowing on Saturday, I'll be leaving. Maybe that's just it. He's a single dad, and I'm a single mom, and maybe, despite him being some famous professional athlete, he's as lonely as I am, and he's looking for some company...temporary company. Can I be that person? I've never been a one-night-stand type of woman. Then again, I barely know what type of woman I am since I've spent all these years focusing on school and Abby. I've had a few short-term relationships, but none of them were ever serious enough to introduce my daughter to.

Maybe, just for this week, I can let myself just be. See where things go... enjoy my time with him for what it is, knowing there's a time limit on it. Or maybe I'm overthinking things, and after tonight, I'll never see Hudson again.

Just as I'm working myself up with the unknowns, another text comes in.

Hudson: And to be clear TBC means I want more time with you. I'll take as many hours of your time while you're here as you'll give me, in any capacity.

Well, okay then. Guess he's not one to beat around the bush. Unsure what to text back, I leave it alone. I'll see him in a couple of hours anyway.

After Abby wakes up from her nap, I give her a quick shower and text Hudson to let him know we're on our way over and to ask for his room number. I find out he's on the top floor, most likely in one of those ridiculous suites, and my suspicions are confirmed when he says he'll meet me downstairs because a special key card is required to access his floor from the elevator.

"Did you leave your kids in the room alone?" I ask when the elevator doors open. He's standing in it alone, dressed in a pair of gray sweats—that should come with a warning label—and a white T-shirt stretched across his chest.

"I don't claim to be an expert in parenting by any means, but even I know not to leave my eight- and five-year-old alone. They'd probably blow something up." He laughs, but his tone conveys he doesn't doubt they would actually do such a thing if left alone.

"You ready to watch a movie?" he asks Abby, who's clinging to my leg.

"Yes," she says softly. "Can we have popcorn too? Mommy and I always have popcorn when we watch movies."

"I think I can make that happen," Hudson tells her with a nod.

"Umm, Hudson. Where are your kids?" I ask. Because if they're not alone, where are they? And then it hits me... "Wait, where were they last night?"

"With Joanie."

The elevator dings, and the doors open. When we step into the hallway, I notice there are only two doors, unlike my floor, which has like fifty.

Hudson places his phone against the door, and it clicks open. "Come on in," he says, swinging it open and letting us pass by.

"Abby!" Presley yells, running out from somewhere. She's freshly dressed, and her hair is done in perfect pigtails. "Come help me choose the movie."

The girls run through the living room and disappear, leaving Hudson and me alone. He steps toward me until we're so close, I can smell his fresh, masculine scent. "I was worried I scared you off with my texts, but I meant what I said. I want to spend more time with you."

"Our time is limited," I say out loud, reminding us both.

"I know," he agrees. "But I've learned the hard way that our time on earth is limited, and instead of worrying about tomorrow, I'd rather just live for right now."

His words are filled with emotion, and I want to ask him what happened to teach him that lesson, but before I can, a woman appears, making me push Hudson away.

"What...?" he begins, and then notices the woman as well. "Joanie, I'd like for you to meet Sawyer. She's Abby's mom."

"Ahh," the woman says, shaking my hand. "I've heard all about Abby...and you." She winks playfully, making Hudson groan under his breath.

"You have?" I ask confused, wondering who the heck this woman is. She seems several years younger than Hudson. Maybe around my age. Could she be his sister? Oh, God, please don't let it be his wife. "And who are you?" I ask, needing to know what I've just walked into. Please don't let it be some weird open marriage arrangement.

"Oh, sorry," Hudson says. "Joanie is Lucas and Presley's nanny. She's with them when I can't be during the season and joins us on the occasional trip. She's been with them since Presley was born."

"It's nice to meet you," I tell her. "Will you be watching the movie with us?"

"Oh, no," she says with a soft laugh. "The bar is playing live music, so I'm going to go check it out. If you need anything..."

"Thanks," Hudson says. "We're good. Enjoy your night."

With a smile, she's out the door, and it's just Hudson and me again.

"Is she staying here with you guys?"

"No, she has her own room next door. I normally don't bring her on family trips, but a few friends mentioned possibly coming down, so I offered her a two-week paid vacation to tag along, and she couldn't resist."

"I don't blame her," I say with a laugh.

Hudson pushes me gently against the counter, his hands caging me in. "I have to admit, her coming along has already come in handy."

"How's that?" I breathe, my body warming at our close contact.

"For one, I was able to stay out all night with you last night..." He stamps a kiss to the corner of my mouth, and my chest tightens in response. "And two, she'll be able to watch all the kids when I ask you out on a date and you say yes."

He presses his lips to mine for a soft, chaste kiss before he pulls back. "So, what do you say, Sawyer? Will you go out with me tomorrow night?"

I mentally shake my head, clearing the lust-filled fog as I try to think of a reason to say no. Because right now, the only word I want to speak is yes, yes, yes. And then I remember...

"I don't have a sitter. My sister and her husband left. They're who watched Abby last night."

"That's what Joanie's for," Hudson replies. "I know you don't know her, but she comes from one of the top nanny services with a background in education. She's trained in CPR and, as I mentioned, has been with my kids for five years."

This time, I actually shake my head. "I don't know..."

"Just think about it," he says, kissing my cheek. "For now, let's go find some popcorn, order dinner, and hope the kids don't pick a movie that's too cheesy."

"Where's Lucas?"

"With the girls, I'm sure."

After we order a bunch of pizzas, drinks, snacks, and popcorn from room service, Hudson takes my hand in his and guides us to wherever the kids are, which turns out to be the theater room. Yes, his suite has an actual room with huge, comfy recliners and a massive projection screen.

"All right, the food's on its way," Hudson announces when we walk inside. "Now, which movie are we watching?"

Of course, all three kids name a different movie.

Five

Hudson

IT'S BEEN FIVE YEARS SINCE I'VE ALLOWED MYSELF TO BE DRAWN to another woman. To pay attention to her luscious curves, her perfect full breasts, to get lost in her lavender scent. I thought when it happened, I would feel guilty, and I was prepared for it. I rehearsed a speech several times over the years to convince myself that it's been long enough, it's okay to move on and be attracted to another woman, but when I kissed Sawyer, it felt as natural as rain. For the first time in years, my heart clenched behind my rib cage, and my dick got excited that I might finally allow him to come out to play.

At first, when I realized I was turned on, all I wanted to do was find an empty bed, peel Sawyer's clothes off her body, and get my dick wet for the first time in five long as fuck years. But the more we talked and got to know one another, the more I wanted... more. More of her truths, of her laughter. More of her smiles. Just fucking more.

When my wife left me, I promised myself I wouldn't become *that guy*. The one who drowns his sorrows in women by having one-night stands to fill the void. I told myself I wouldn't degrade what we had by becoming some manwhore. The problem is, when you're raising two kids and live in the type of world I live in, it's damn near impossible to meet a woman with any substance, who I could see myself having a future with. So, one year turned into two, and two turned into four, and the next thing I knew, I'd spent the past five years focusing on football and my kids without even attempting to be with another woman since my wife.

"I should probably take Abby back to our room," Sawyer rasps as the credits roll, and I run my palm up her smooth thigh. She's wearing tiny cotton shorts and a tank that show off her sexy body and tan, and I can't stop touching her. It's been this way the entire movie. The kids sprawled out across the first row of chairs with pillows and blankets, so Sawyer and I sat behind them. With a blanket draped over us, I spent the movie running my hand along her flesh, teasing the apex of her thighs but never taking it any further.

"Or she can spend the night," I whisper, turning the movie off, then leaning in and catching her earlobe between my teeth. She shivers under my touch, and I chuckle at how responsive she is. "The kids are passed out. Let them have a sleepover while we have one of our own."

She turns her face to look at me, and the desire in her eyes has me wanting to ravish the hell out of her. "What if they wake up?" She chews on her bottom lip nervously, and I know, despite how much we want each other, taking it further can't happen with the kids in the same room.

"How about we move this to the living room?" I suggest.

She nods in agreement, and we quietly exit the theater room, leaving the kids asleep. When we get to the living room, I open a bottle of white wine and pour her a glass, then make myself a whiskey.

"I'm sorry," she says, accepting the glass from me and taking a sip.

"You don't have to apologize." I sit next to her, and she snuggles in close to me. "The truth is I haven't been with a woman in several years."

She pulls back slightly, her eyes going wide. "Really? Why?"

"I haven't been with anyone since my wife died," I admit for the first time to anyone. Over the years, I've been occasionally seen with a different woman on my arm at social events, but none of them had me wanting more, not like Sawyer does.

She gasps, her hand covering her mouth. "Your wife died?"

It's public knowledge, but since she didn't know who I was, it makes sense that she doesn't know about my personal past. I also love that her not knowing means she didn't Google me.

"She died two days after she gave birth to Presley. Fluid embolism. A rare but deadly complication. One minute, she was holding our daughter, and the next, she was gone.

We did everything the way we were supposed to. Met at a charity event and started dating. I was a few years into my career, and she had recently graduated from college with her master's and was working at her father's company. A year after dating, I proposed, and a year after that, we were married. Two years later, Lucas came, and a couple years after that, we decided to have a second child. Three years apart, according to her, was the perfect age difference."

I sigh and rest my elbows on my knees, scrubbing my face with my hands. "I'm sorry. I've never had to explain this to anyone, and now that I am, it's fucking hard."

She takes my hand in hers and brings it up to her heart. "I can't even imagine."

"It wasn't supposed to happen like that," I tell her, my throat clogged with emotion. "We were supposed to raise our family together. She became a stay-at-home mom when Lucas was born, and when she died..." I sigh in frustration. "I try so damn hard. But I'll never be her. I'm trying to do it all, but since she died, it feels like I've been failing over and over again."

I glance up at her and blink away the tears threatening.

"My kids have spent more time with Joanie than me between practices and traveling during the season. Then add in the endorsements and functions. My contract ended, and they asked me to re-sign for three years, but I don't know if I can do it. They needed an answer like yesterday, so I disappeared and came here."

"Your kids are well taken care of," she says, moving closer so our bodies are touching. "There's nothing wrong with a single parent working to support his kids. On many nights, I cried myself to sleep feeling guilty over studying instead of playing with Abby. I want to give her the world, but I also need to be able to feed her. You're having working parent guilt, but that's not fair. I've only been around your kids a little while, but it's clear they love you and are close to you. Hell, they're both practically a mini version of you." She laughs, breaking the tension, and I find myself smiling because everything she says makes sense.

"Where's Abby's father?" I ask, being nosy. But based on what she said, he must not be around.

She blows out a harsh breath. "Unlike you and…"

"Clara."

"Unlike you and Clara, we did everything wrong." She chuckles self-deprecatingly. "We started dating our senior year of high school, had unprotected sex, and I got pregnant. He promised to be there for me, and at first, he was, but then he and his band got picked up by a label, and he took off. I caught him cheating on me several times and ended things. I was hoping maybe he'd get it together when Abby was born, but when he found out they were going to sign a huge record deal, he signed his rights away, so he wouldn't be responsible for paying child support." She shrugs like it's no big deal while I fist my hands, wanting to find the asshole and wring his neck.

"It's for the best," she says. "Abby never knew him, so she couldn't miss him. His band was a one-hit wonder. He's probably living off the little bit of money they made and has never tried to contact us."

"He's an idiot," I tell her, palming the side of her face in my hand. "He has no idea what he's missing out on not knowing you two."

She smiles softly, and I lean in and kiss her. My tongue pushes through the seam of her lips, and she moans into my mouth. The kiss quickly turns heated as I hover over her, tasting her, devouring her.

My hand finds her breast, and I pinch her nipple through her shirt. Her back arches in pleasure, silently begging for more, so I do it again, this time harder. I worry I'm going to hurt her, and for a split second, my thoughts go to my wife—Clara liked it soft and gentle, always. But then Sawyer breathes, "More," against my mouth, and I shake her from my head. I'm here with Sawyer, and she deserves to have one hundred percent of me.

Sliding my hand under her top, I pull her bra cup down and tweak her nipple until she screams out in pleasure-pain.

"Yes, just like that," she hisses, wrapping and tightening her legs around my waist. "It feels so good."

I lift her shirt up enough to expose her pert pink nipple and dip my head. Taking it between my teeth, I alternate between biting and sucking on it. Her hands go to my short hair, and she tugs on the ends as I expose her other nipple and give it the same attention.

"Oh, God," she breathes. "Please don't stop." Her hot center grinds against me, and I need to know what she feels like. If she's as turned on as I am.

Leaving her shorts on, I peel them, along with her underwear, to the side and thrust a finger into her, finding her soaking wet. I add another digit and finger-fuck her while my thumb massages her clit. Within seconds, she detonates around my fingers, screaming my name in ecstasy. I quickly release her nipple from my lips and crush my mouth against hers, swallowing down her cries as she comes long and hard.

Only when she's finally quiet and sighs into me do I stop kissing and fingering her. I pull back slightly and can't help the grin on my face as I take in her flushed cheeks and sated gaze.

"What?" she murmurs, stretching out, her lashes fluttering open and shut in contentment.

"It's been a while, and I was worried I was rusty. Good to know I still got it." I shrug, then cringe because I'm pretty sure inadvertently bringing up my sex life with my dead wife isn't the best way to follow up giving a woman an orgasm.

Thankfully, Sawyer snorts out a laugh and opens her eyes, shaking her head. "I can't speak for what you *had*, but if it was this level of skill, you definitely still have it...at least your fingers do." She winks playfully, and I scoop her up, ready to show her my dick still has it too. Only before we make it to my room, the sound of Presley calling my name halts me in my place.

"Daddy!" Presley yells again, making me jump into action.

"Put me down!" Sawyer whisper-yells, reminding me she's still in my arms.

"Sorry," I say with a laugh. "I couldn't figure out which head to think with."

She barks out a laugh and shoves past me into the room where Abby and Lucas are still fast asleep and Presley is sitting up, scrubbing her eyes.

"I'm thirsty," she mutters, still half-asleep.

"I better take Abby back to our room," Sawyer says while I grab Presley a drink.

"No, it's late. Stay the night, please." When she side-eyes me, I raise my hands in a placating manner. "I don't want you walking in the dark alone, and Joanie isn't here to watch the kids so I can walk you back."

"Fine, but we're not sleeping together. I'll sleep on the couch."

"You can have the bed," I insist.

After Presley drinks her water, I pick her up and carry her to her room—only after she begs for Abby to sleep in her bed too. It's kind of cute how quickly the girls have become such good friends. Once both girls are tucked in and Lucas is fast asleep in his bed, I walk Sawyer to my room, so I can use the bathroom.

"You know," she says when I come out from brushing my teeth. "Just because we can't sleep together doesn't mean I can't return the favor." She reaches for my dick, but I back up, not liking the sound of that.

"What?" she asks, a look of confusion marring her beautiful features.

"What I did to you wasn't a favor. And it's certainly not one that has to be reciprocated."

Her face falls, and I hate that I've upset her. "Hey," I say, tilting her chin up to look at me. "If you want to crawl into that bed and make out with me like a couple of horny teenagers, I'm down. And if you want to touch me, I'm completely okay with that, but please don't feel like you're obligated to do anything."

She stares at me for a long second, and I fear I've fucked up by overthinking shit. But it's hard not to when you've lived in a world where everyone is out for themselves and the only reason they think of anyone else is to get ahead. I've had dozens of women come on to me over the past five years, but they all want the same thing—a piece of my fame. It's hard to get out of that mindset, even knowing Sawyer isn't like that. That she isn't doing something out of obligation because of who I am.

"Hudson." She frames my face and, lifting on her tiptoes, kisses the corner of my mouth. "I don't feel obligated in any way." She peppers my stubbled jaw with kisses, then moves to my neck and collarbone. "Since last night, I've been dying to explore this body. Making you feel good is just a bonus." She winks playfully, then lifts my shirt over my head, and presses kisses to my chest and down my torso.

When she's on her knees, looking up at me with a mischievous grin on her face, she places an open-mouthed kiss to the bulge under my sweats, and my dick thickens, knowing what's to come. I glance behind her and notice, at some point while I was in the bathroom, she closed the door.

She rubs her lips over my material-covered dick until it's stretching my briefs, then she tugs them down, springing my dick free. My eyes stay trained on her as she strokes my hard shaft up and down a few times until it's as hard as stone. Her tongue darts out and drags along the top of my head, then she opens her perfect mouth and takes me all the way down her throat.

"Jesus Christ," I hiss, watching her head go up and down as she sucks my dick. Her mouth is warm and wet, and when she suctions her cheeks, tightening her hold on my shaft, I damn near come right on the spot. It's been too long, and it feels too good.

Her hands grip my sides, her fingers digging into my flesh, and she starts to fuck me with her mouth. In the otherwise quiet room, the sound of her slurping and sucking fills the air, and I know I won't last long. I don't want it to end like this. I want to be inside her, over her, kissing her, and feeling her insides, but with the kids in the other room and not wanting to chance them waking up and knocking on the door, I know that can't happen tonight.

When I'm about to come, I tug on Sawyer's hair to pull

her off me, planning to finish in my hand or maybe on her chest. But she swats me away, silently demanding I finish in her mouth. I want to argue, but I'm too far gone, so I let myself go, coming straight down her throat. She takes it all, not stopping until I'm flaccid and she's licked every drop off my shaft.

When she's done, she glances up at me shyly. "So... do I still have it? I was worried about being rusty."

I throw my head back with a laugh, then give her the same answer she gave me. "I don't know what you *had*, but based on how hard I just came, you definitely still have it."

Six

Sawyer

"IS PRESLEY GOING TO CAMP?" ABBY ASKS AS I HAND HER A
bathing suit to put on.

"Nope."

"Is Lucas going to camp?" she asks, peeling her clothes off
so she can get changed.

"Nope," I repeat.

"Because we're in trouble?" She pulls her suit up her tiny
body and wiggles to get the straps on.

"No," I tell her, helping to fix it so the material is where
it should be before I hand over her cover-up. "Nobody's in

trouble. Hudson invited us to spend the day with them, so instead of going to camp, we're going to hang out with them."

"So, Lucas and Presley will both be there?" she confirms.

"Yes."

"Can I go to camp tomorrow?"

"We'll see."

She glares my way, hating that answer. "Fine. Can we go see Presley and Lucas now?"

"As soon as I get my bathing suit on, we're going to meet them downstairs."

"Okay, Mommy, then hurry up." Abby pushes me toward the bathroom to get ready while I laugh at how crazy she is. She's never made friends so quickly before, and I'm a little worried about how she'll react when our vacation is over and we have to say goodbye.

I probably should create some space, so it's not so hard, but I don't want to ruin our time simply because I'm afraid of the after-effects. It's not fair to Abby, and if I'm honest, I'm really enjoying my time with Hudson even though it's temporary.

Last night, it was hard to sleep in his bed, knowing he

was in the other room on the couch. It would've been so easy to sneak him back into the room, lock the door, and—

"Mommy! Hurry," Abby huffs with impatience. "What if they leave without us?"

"They're not leaving without us." I snag my suit and change into it. Today, I'm wearing a one-piece black suit with see-through triangle cut-outs on the sides. It's cute and practical. Hudson wouldn't tell me what we were doing, aside from saying to make sure we pack bathing suits and a change of clothes and towels.

After I have our beach bag packed, I text Hudson to let him know we're ready, and then we head downstairs to meet them in front of our building. The second the girls see each other, they run straight into each other's arms like it's been years instead of hours since they last saw each other.

"What's on the agenda for today?" I ask Hudson.

"The boat!" Lucas answers for him. "Dad rented the best boat ever, and we get to ride on the back on the tube."

"I'm not riding on the tube," Presley says. "It's too scary. Last time, I almost flew off."

"I don't like scary," Abby adds.

Lucas pouts. "You guys are no fun. Will you ride with me, Sawyer? Dad can't because he has to drive the boat." He looks up at me with such hope that even if I was scared shitless, I would still agree to go. Luckily, I've been tubing countless times on the lake.

"Sounds like fun. I'm there."

"Yes!" Lucas extends his arm for a fist bump.

When we arrive at the marina, the man in charge immediately recognizes Hudson. Once he's done fanguying hard, he gives him exceptionally good service, asking him no less than a dozen times if he needs anything. Hudson handles it like the pro he is, asking him to please not mention he's here, and offers to sign a bunch of crap while I try like hell to refrain from laughing. Maybe it's because I'm not into sports, or because I only know Hudson as... well, Hudson—the man I met at the bar and fell for, the single dad who loves his kids. I can't imagine reacting that way over a man who throws a ball for a living, but that's just me.

The boat is perfect with several seats for the kids, and once we get their lifejackets clipped on, Hudson takes off out of the marina, heading down the Intracoastal. The area is beautiful, and while the kids sit up front, laughing as the boat creates a spray of water mixed with the breeze, I take pictures of everything around me.

"Come here," Hudson says, jutting his chin downward.

"Yes?"

He pulls me in front of him, my back to his chest, and cages me in with his arms. Where we're positioned, we can see the kids, and if they happened to look back, they can see us too.

"Have I told you today how beautiful you look?" he murmurs into my ear, sneaking a quick kiss to the curve of my neck. Shivers rush through me, and my legs clench in want.

"You haven't," I breathe out, shaking my head.

"Well, you do. This bathing suit..." He glides his fingers along the see-through material just under the curve of my breast. "It's like the biggest damn tease. So close, yet so damn far..."

"Are we still on for tonight?" I ask, keeping my eye on the kids.

"Damn right, we are. I'm counting down the minutes."

His hand moves downward, but before he can touch me there, I dip under his arm and out of his hold.

"Down, boy." I wink. "There are children in our presence."

Hudson chuckles under his breath. "I can't help myself. I lose all self-control when I'm around you."

"Dad, when can we go on the tube?" Lucas yells.

"Soon."

"Have you done this before?" I ask when we're situated in the middle of the water, and Lucas and I are holding on to the handles of the tube behind the boat. I probably should've asked before I got on the tube, but too late now.

"Of course," he says with a laugh.

"Dad has two boats," Lucas informs me.

"Ready?" Hudson yells.

"Yeah!" we both shout back.

The boat takes off slowly, speeding up little by little until the wind is whipping around us and the water is spritzing our faces.

"Faster, Dad!" Lucas yells, making me laugh.

We ride the mini waves for several minutes behind the boat, bringing me momentarily back to my teenage years at the lake. The days before I was forced to become a responsible adult. When Abby's sperm donor, Joey, and I were younger. The boat was faster, and we were reckless, drinking and smoking and partying without a care in the world.

The day I found out I was pregnant, my entire life changed. Everything came to a standstill. I'll never for a second regret having my daughter—she's my entire universe, the moon, and the stars—but at this moment, as Lucas whoops and hollers, I realize that while Joey was wrong, refusing to slow down even a tad, becoming a mom didn't mean I had to stop living altogether.

"TWO BURGERS, CHICKEN TENDERS, AND A MAHI SANDWICH," Hudson parrots our orders. "All right, I'll be back in a few minutes."

After a few hours of fun in the sun, we've docked the boat at a restaurant on the island to have lunch and use the bathroom.

"Can we go play?" Presley asks me once her dad has gone

up to the bar to place our order. Instead of eating at a table, the kids asked if we could picnic near the playground.

"Sure, just stay in that area," I tell them even though I have no intention of removing my eyes from where they're going. It's different keeping an eye on three kids instead of one, especially when mine barely leaves my side.

I'm watching them play what looks like tag when Lucas barrels down the sidewalk to catch his sister and faceplants on the concrete. Instinctively, I leap out of my seat, running straight for him as he sits up, blood coating his mouth and tears leaking out of his eyes.

"Come here." I pull him into my arms, even though he's heavy, and carry him back to the blanket, calling for the girls to follow me.

"Mommy, he's bleeding!" Abby points out.

"I know, sweetie." I set Lucas down and grab my bag, which has a first-aid kit in it. Luckily, the fall looked worse than it was, and aside from a bleeding lip, the rest of him is okay. "It's going to sting, but we need to clean it up to see how bad it is, okay?" I say to Lucas. He's trying so hard to remain strong, but his trembling lip and tear-filled lids give away how badly he's hurt.

He nods once, and I wipe his mouth gently, making sure he doesn't get scraped by any rocks or debris.

"It hurts," he mumbles.

"It's okay," Abby says, taking his hand in hers. "Mommy will make it better. That's what mommies do. Right, Mommy?"

I nod, and at the same time, Lucas stiffens under me.

"I don't have a mom," Presley says as I clean the area of the cut. Thankfully, it's not deep, so it won't need stitches.

"Yes, you do," Lucas argues. "She's just in heaven."

"Where's that?" Abby asks in confusion.

"Where people go when they die," Lucas answers. "In the clouds."

Abby's mouth falls open as her head tilts to the sky. "I don't have a daddy. Is he in the clouds too?"

Oh, Lord, help me. "No, he's not in the sky," I tell her, praying she'll let it go. Now is not the time to have *that* conversation. She's never asked about her lack of a father, but I told myself I would be ready with the perfect response once she does.

"There," I say to Lucas, once the butterfly stitches have closed the cut and the bleeding has stopped. "All better."

His glassy eyes meet mine, and he sniffles away his tears. "Thank you."

"What happened?" Hudson asks, dropping the bags of food to the blanket and enveloping his son into his arms with concern.

"I was running and fell," Lucas tells him. "Sawyer fixed it."

"It's just a small cut. I cleaned and bandaged it."

Hudson sighs in relief and hugs his son as though he's his lifeline. When he releases him, he pulls me into a side hug and kisses my temple. "Thank you for taking care of my boy."

"Can we eat now?" Presley asks, grabbing one of the brown bags. "I'm hungry."

After we eat, we walk through the shops, have ice cream for dessert, and then get back on the boat. The kids are lounging in the front while I'm hanging in the back with Hudson, chatting, when Abby stands on her seat.

I rush forward, fearing she's going to fall over, as she points at the pod of dolphins just up ahead. "Mommy! I want to swim with them," she begs, jumping up and down.

"You can't stand while the boat is going," I chide, pulling her off the seat and onto the floor where she's safe. Hudson had turned off the boat the second she stood, and it's idling in place.

"I'm sorry, but I want to swim with them! Please."

The dolphins continue to glide in and out of the water as if they're putting on a show.

"Please. Please." Her bottom lip juts out, and I laugh at how adorable she is.

"Can we swim with them, please?" Presley joins in.

"You could if you went tubing," Lucas points out to the girls, who both shake their heads.

"Did someone say they want to swim with the dolphins?" Hudson says, walking over and pulling his shirt off and exposing his body. My lady parts tingle, and I'm forced to look away before I'm caught drooling.

"We do!" The girls both raise their hands.

"All right, but we can't get too close because dolphins get scared."

"Yay!" the girls cheer.

Hudson drops the tube into the water, and the girls look at him wearily. "Your chariot has arrived," he says, dramatically bowing. "And I'm your chauffeur." He places the girls into the center of the tube and then turns to Lucas. "You coming?"

"My lip still kind of hurts," he says. "Can I stay here?"

"Of course," I tell him. "I'll stay with you."

Hudson jumps into the water and takes off swimming, pulling the girls on the tube behind him. The dolphins have disappeared, and Abby yells, "Come back, dolphins. Come swimming with us," while she reaches into the water, paddling like she's actually swimming.

I pull my phone out to snap pictures as Hudson pulls them around the boat in a circle. The girls giggle, and even though it's doubtful they're going to actually get to swim with the dolphins, they're having a blast.

"Hey, look!" Lucas shouts, pointing straight ahead.

"Dolphins!" the girls screech in excitement. I take several more pictures as Hudson swims near the dolphins, who shockingly don't take off right away, giving the girls enough time to feel like they're actually swimming with them.

When Hudson swims back, he pulls the tube close and ties it up before helping each girl back into the boat. We look at the pictures I took, and they name each of the dolphins while swearing they were smiling and swimming with them.

Lucas rolls his eyes, and Hudson chuckles as he dries off and then goes back to the wheel to take off again. I leave the girls counting how many dolphins there are and walk over to join him, wrapping my arms around his waist. "Thank you," I murmur, looking up at him. "You just made my daughter's day."

He glances down at me. "How about her mother? What would it take to make her day?"

"Seeing my daughter happy makes my day."

He nods in understanding and dips his head to kiss my forehead. "Maybe tonight we can work on what makes *you* happy."

Seven

Hudson

"WHERE ARE YOU GOING, DAD?" PRESLEY ASKS WHEN SHE WALKS into my room in her pajamas and sees I'm dressed in a pair of khaki pants and a collared shirt—not my usual attire during our stay at the beach. I consider lying to her since this is all new and I haven't been on a date since her mom passed away, but I go for the truth because I promised myself I'd always be honest with my children.

"I'm going to take Sawyer out to dinner."

She tilts her head to the side slightly in thought. "Like on a date?"

"Yes, like on a date."

"Will she be your girlfriend?"

I chuckle at her question. "No, we're just friends." It's a little white lie, but not really because come Saturday, when it's time for Sawyer and Abby to check out and leave, all that will be left is our friendship and memories.

Presley nods thoughtfully. "You should make her your girlfriend. She's pretty and nice."

"That she is," I agree.

"Is Abby coming over to sleep?" she asks, changing the subject.

"Yeah. Joanie is going to watch you guys tonight." I check the time on my watch. "They should be here soon."

"Hey, Dad!" Lucas calls out. "Can we go to camp tomorrow? It's snorkeling day."

I walk out to the kitchen, where he's checking out the calendar of events. "Of course." I ruffle his hair. "Is your lip good enough to go in the salt water?"

He runs his tongue along the Band-Aid-covered flesh and nods. "Yeah, I'm tough."

"Yeah, you are. You want to go too?" I ask Presley.

Before she can answer, there's a knock on our door. I wanted to pick Sawyer up like a proper date, but she told me that's ridiculous when she has to drop Abby off.

I open the door, and Abby rushes in, dressed in her pajamas with a backpack on. "Hey, Presley." She waves. "I brought some coloring books. Do you like to color?"

"Yeah!"

Lucas comes out with his snorkel on, making everyone laugh. "You planning to go snorkeling in the bathtub?" Sawyer asks.

"No," Lucas replies seriously. "I'm trying it on for tomorrow. It's snorkeling day at camp."

"I have a pink one," Presley adds, running off to grab it so she can show everyone.

"Am I going snorkeling too?" Abby asks her mom. "I don't have a snorkel."

"No, sweetie. Your group is going to collect seashells and go on a wildlife boat tour." Abby and Presley are in the same group, while Lucas is in a group with older kids.

Presley comes back with her pink snorkel in hand. "Wait, we're not going snorkeling?" She scrunches her nose up in disapproval.

"No," Lucas tells her. "You're too young. Only my group is going."

"That's not fair." Presley pouts, crossing her arms over her chest.

"But we get to pick up pretty shells," Abby tells her.

"But I wanna go snorkeling."

"How about we go tomorrow after camp?" I offer. "We can buy Abby and Sawyer snorkels and all go together."

"Fine," Presley says. "Let's go color."

She grabs Abby's arm and is about to drag her away, but Sawyer stops her first.

"You're sure you're okay with Joanie watching you?" she asks softly, bending so she's at her daughter's level. Joanie's been around the past couple of days, so Abby and Sawyer have met her and are comfortable with her. She's the best damn nanny, and I dread the day she decides to start her own family and quits. She's dated a few guys off and on, but nothing serious.

"Yeah." Abby kisses her mom and then runs off with Presley.

"I'll let Joanie know we're leaving," I tell Sawyer, pulling my phone out of my pocket and shooting her a text.

"Can I rent a movie?" Lucas asks.

"Sure, bud. But make sure Joanie approves it first, please."

"Thanks! Bye, Dad! Bye, Sawyer!" Lucas sprints out of the room just as Joanie walks in.

"Hey, Sawyer. You look pretty. I love that dress."

"Thanks. My sister bought it for me at one of the shops on the island."

I glance at Sawyer, having been too busy with the kids to take her in. She's dressed in a peach wraparound dress with a low front that draws attention to her ample cleavage, and the short length shows off her tanned, toned legs. She's wearing white strappy sandals, and her toes are freshly painted the same color as her dress. Her hair is down in loose waves, and she's wearing some makeup.

"You look beautiful," I tell her, taking her hand in mine and pulling her into my arms since the kids are nowhere in sight. "I should've told you that when you first got here. I'm sorry."

"Eh." She waves me off playfully. "All in the life of a

parent." She shrugs. "You clean up well." She runs her palm along my freshly shaven face. "But I have to admit, I like the scruff."

"I'll never shave again," I joke, making Joanie laugh.

"I'm going to check on the kids," she says. "Have fun."

We take the elevator down, and I grab my car from the valet since I've made reservations at a restaurant on the other side of the island. We're both quiet for several minutes before I decide to break the silence. My time with Sawyer is limited, and I need to make the most of it.

"Would you rather have a life rewind button or a life pause button?" She glances over at me and raises a single brow. "My parents used to play this game during long car rides."

"Are you close with your parents?" she asks.

"Yeah, for the most part. My dad played in the NFL too. Retired many years ago, and they live in Florida most of the year. But they have a place in New York as well to visit the kids and me. I'm an only child, so my kids are pretty spoiled."

"Wow, two football players in the family? That's crazy."

"It's actually common. When your dad is good, they're

more likely to follow your game as well. What about you? Are you close with your parents?"

"Too close," she mutters, but the quirk of her lips tells me she isn't as unhappy about that as she's making it seem. "I live with them. When Joey left me high and dry, they offered to let me move in rent-free as long as I promised to go to college. It was an offer I couldn't refuse. They've been my rock, especially since my brother and sister flew the coop years ago and haven't returned."

"Moral support is important. I don't know what I would've done without my parents when Clara died. Presley was born right in the middle of the season. We were undefeated. I thought Clara would give birth, and then I'd go back to work..."

"Did you go back?"

I swallow the lump of emotion down. I started it, so it's only fair I finish, but it's hard to go back to those days. "Yeah, I did. And I got a lot of shit for it. I could've pulled out, terminated my contract. My wife had just died. But I couldn't do it. I took two weeks off, and then another since it was a bye week. And then I returned. We won the Super

Bowl that year."

But my wife was still dead, and my newborn daughter and three-year-old son spent more time with Joanie than they did with me.

Sawyer's hand slides into mine, lacing her fingers with mine, and the small gesture feels really fucking big. "A lot of people who are heartbroken get lost in their work. Joey cheating on me and then signing over his rights to our daughter hurt like a bitch. I cried for weeks wondering why we weren't enough for him. And then to push it away, I got lost in school."

"How did we go from playing *would you rather* to something so deep?" I joke, not wanting the night to take a dark turn.

"We never started playing." She laughs, and the sound has my insides knotting.

I pull up to the valet and exchange my keys and a tip for a ticket, and then we head inside. The restaurant is on the water, and I've requested outdoor seating. The hostess welcomes us and takes us to the table. Sawyer orders a dirty martini, and I order a Coke since I'm driving.

"I'd rather press a pause life button," she says out of nowhere. It takes me a second to remember what I asked her for my *would you rather* question. "Life right now feels pretty damn good. I'm a college graduate. I have a job. This vacation has been the perfect mix of fun and relaxing. Abby's met some new friends. I've met you." Her eyes lock with mine. "It feels like for the first time I can finally breathe easy."

"I completely understand what you mean."

"So, is it my turn now?" she asks after the waiter has taken our order. "Do I get to ask you a question?"

"Yep."

She taps her chin and looks up at the sky in mock concentration. "Okay, I got one." The devilish smirk on her face has me thinking she's about to ask me something crazy, and a few seconds later, she confirms my suspicions. "Would you rather get caught having sex by your kids or by your parents?"

She waggles her brows and giggles, and holy hell, I'm a goner.

"My parents. No contest. Hands down. They were all over each other growing up, and I walked in on them too many times to count. I'm scarred for life." I visibly shiver. "It would be payback for sure."

She throws her head back in a laugh, and my gaze goes straight to her slim neck, wanting to lick my way down her flesh so I can taste every inch of her.

"My turn." I clear my throat. "Would you rather have one weekend of the best sex of your life or a lifetime of shitty sex?"

She sobers, looking thoughtful. "One weekend."

I'm shocked by her words. "Really?"

"Yeah. Because if it's shitty, it's because we're not connected on a deeper level. There's no chemistry, no spark. I want the ripping clothes off because we can't keep our hands and bodies to ourselves, mind-blowing, explosive sex. The kind of sex that leaves you out of breath and your body buzzing. The connection that grips the organ in your chest and tugs on your heartstrings, reminding you that you're alive and life is for the taking. I would rather experience *that* kind of sex for only a weekend than never be given the chance to feel it at all."

Her passionate words damn near knock the breath out

of me. "Have you ever felt it?" I ask, leaning in closer to her.

She shakes her head. "Not yet. I've experienced the fumbling teenage sex, the I'm comfortable with you sex, the hate sex, the make-up sex, the awkward it's not going anywhere sex, but never the explosive, chemistry-filled, life-altering sex."

"That's a lot of sex," I joke.

She shrugs. "A lot of it was with the same guy."

"If you've never experienced it, then how do you know it exists?"

She sucks her bottom lip into her mouth as she considers my question. "I guess I don't know if it does," she says thoughtfully. "But you asked which one I'd rather have." She shrugs. "I'll take a weekend of real over a lifetime of fake... because the fake, now *that*, I know firsthand."

Hudson

"WHEW!" SAWYER BREATHES OUT, SHAKING HER HEAD AS WE both slam our shot glasses on the bar. "That's some strong shit." She giggles, I'm sure feeling the effects of the whiskey shots we've been shooting between dances. Letting loose has been the perfect nightcap for our date. When she mentioned after dinner that she wanted to go to the hotel bar where we first met, I was worried maybe she was having second thoughts about us spending the night together. But the way she's been grinding her delectable body against mine as if we're the only two people on the dance floor has me thinking she's not doubting anything.

"Another one?" I raise my hand to call the bartender over, but Sawyer places her hand on mine.

"No, I think I've had enough." Her heated gaze locks with mine. "Let's go back to my room."

She doesn't have to tell me twice. Since the tab is linked to my room, I link our fingers together and pull her through the bar toward the exit. I don't realize how fast I'm walking until she cracks up, tugging on my hand.

"I can't walk that fast!" She laughs. "You've got like a foot on me."

"Well, then, I'll just have to help you." I lift her over my shoulder, smacking her ass as I stalk through the hotel.

"Hudson!" she shrieks through her laughter. "Put me down, you big goof!" She swats at my ass, but I ignore her, continuing on my way, not giving a shit that everyone is probably looking at us. I blame it on the whiskey shots.

As I'm passing the resort store, Sawyer smacks my ass again. "Hudson, put me down. I need to go by the store."

I stop in my place. "For what?"

"Just put me down," she breathes.

I do as she says, and once she's upright, her face flushed and her eyes shining with laughter, I can't help but pull her into my arms and kiss the hell out of her. She moans into my mouth, and her arms snake around my neck. We kiss like this for several beats before she pulls back slightly.

"Do you have any condoms?" she whispers against my lips, making me stiffen in response.

"I…"

"I didn't think so," she says with a smirk.

"What's that supposed to mean?" I ask as she drags her hands down my chest and stands on her tiptoes to kiss my jawline.

"It means, you mentioned you haven't had sex in five years, so it would make sense you don't have any condoms. And the fact that you don't is a hell of a turn-on. Because that means you weren't planning to get laid." She kisses my pulse point, sucking softly on my flesh. "And since it's been some time since I've had sex, I'm not on birth control, which means we need condoms."

She fists the front of my shirt and pulls me into the store, not stopping until we're standing in the small area that houses feminine products, diapers, and condoms. I laugh lightly at the irony of this aisle.

"What?" Sawyer asks, glancing at me.

"Nothing. I've just always found it funny that no matter what, you're heading to this aisle for something. Even at the resort store, it's all on the same aisle."

She takes the aisle in with new eyes, and when it all clicks, she barks out a laugh. "Oh my God, I never noticed that."

We step in front of the condoms, and since she's still tipsy, she starts naming them all out loud. "We have pleasure pack... Hmm, that sounds good to me." She winks dramatically. "Or how about extra sensitive..." She waggles her brows. "Oh! Look at this one. For her pleasure. Now, that's what I'm talking about." She goes to grab the pack, but I slap her hand away and twirl her around, lifting her into my arms and kissing her hard.

"You stay here," I tell her when I set her on her feet.

She giggles but listens.

The selection is limited since we're at a resort, so I quickly grab a box and am about to head to the register when Sawyer snatches them from my hands. "Magnum large size condoms BareSkin," she reads out loud with a wide grin on her face.

"What?"

"Nothing, I agree." She shrugs. "You are large. I could barely fit you in my—"

I cover her mouth with my hands playfully. "No more talking for you," I say and then drag her to the front of the store to check out. Thankfully, the cashier rings me up quickly, and we're back at her place a few minutes later.

The second we step through the door, Sawyer jumps into my arms, her legs winding around my torso and her arms circling my neck. Her mouth crashes fervently against mine, and I kiss her back just as deep and fierce.

With our mouths connected, I walk us through her hotel room, straight to her bedroom, and lay her on the bed. We break apart only long enough to tear each other's clothes off, and then go back to kissing. Our tongues entwining and tasting, our mouths stroking and coaxing. She tastes like whiskey and something that's just her, and I know I could easily become addicted to her.

I end the kiss so I can taste other parts of her. Her neck

and collarbone are slim, and her skin is soft. When I suck on her flesh, she shivers in response, so I do it again and again. Her legs tighten around me, and she moans into my ear, nipping on my lobe.

I move down to her perfect breasts, massaging them first and then dropping my head to take her rose-dusted nipples into my mouth, licking and sucking on them. Remembering how rough Sawyer liked it, I take one between my teeth and bite on it, tugging hard and then licking away the sting. She moans loudly, and the sound goes straight to my dick.

I trail kisses along her tight stomach she told me she works hard to keep and end at her neatly trimmed pussy. I spread her legs and inhale her lavender-mixed-with-the-ocean scent, wanting to bottle it up for later so I never forget the smell.

I lick her clit, devouring her until she's coming apart under me, writhing and panting my name, begging me to fuck her. Our eyes meet, and she drags me over her. Her tongue darts out and licks my lips, tasting herself on me. And then our mouths connect, and like metal shoved into a socket, sparks like nothing I've ever felt before zap through my body.

My dick is hard against her thigh, and she grabs it in her hand, stroking it softly. I want to be inside her, and I'm about to be when I remember we need a condom.

Breaking our contact, I reach for the box of condoms she dropped on the nightstand. I try to tear it open and notice my hands are shaking slightly. It's been a long time since I've done this, and a million worries fill my head. *What if I'm not good? What if I don't last?* She'll be disappointed...The last woman I was with was my—

As if sensing my inner turmoil, Sawyer sits up and places her hand over mine, gently taking the condom packet from me. "Lie down," she says softly, taking charge, and hell, if that doesn't make me fall for her that much more.

I do as she says, lying on my back with my head resting against the headboard. She rips the packet open and climbs onto the bed, straddling my thighs. With my dick in her hand, she rolls the latex carefully over my shaft and then leans over to give it an open-mouthed kiss. The action sends another jolt of electricity through my body, this time going straight to my heart. I've spent years focusing on everyone else, picking up the slack my late wife left behind and feeling guilty for not doing it as good as she would've.

And because I was too lost in my own guilt and grief, I put up a wall, refusing to let anyone else in. Yet, somehow, in the short time I've known Sawyer, she's not only climbed over that wall but she's also ripped my chest cavity apart and has found a direct line to my heart.

Sawyer climbs up, resting her hands on my shoulders, and I hold her hips as she lowers herself onto me. Her tight pussy sucks my dick in, little by little, until I'm seated all the way inside her. I close my eyes momentarily as the guilt of being inside a woman who isn't my late wife overtakes me. She's dead, and I know this, but that doesn't stop the shame from coming just the same.

"Hudson," Sawyer murmurs, her lips pressing against mine. "Stay with me, please."

Her soft plea has me opening my eyes and meeting her bright green gaze. Her long brown hair is spilling over us, creating a barrier to block out the world around us.

It's just Sawyer and me...in this bed together, our bodies connected as one. I exhale a slow, calming breath, releasing my guilt at the same time, telling myself that I can have this. I deserve this. I've worked hard. I've taken care of my kids. I've spent years feeling alone, and it's okay to let someone in, to allow my heart to feel again.

She starts moving, rising and falling, fucking me slow and deep. I fist her hair, pulling her face to mine so I can kiss her, taste her. Our mouths make love to the same rhythm our bodies do—possessively, desperately.

As she cries out her orgasm, her walls tightening around me, I fly over the edge with her, draining my release into the condom, though I secretly wish nothing was between us. That my seed was coating her insides instead, filling her up.

Sawyer doesn't pull off me right away. Instead, she rains kisses all over my face and neck, and I love that she doesn't want to break our connection. Because I crave her just as much and need her just as hard. I want her in a way I've never wanted anyone else in my life.

The last thought has my insides turning cold, my wall of guilt erecting, and I scramble to lift her off me and go straight to the bathroom to remove the condom and clean up. When I walk back out, she's sitting on the bed, staring at the door with her teeth trapping her bottom lip.

"What's wrong?" she asks softly.

"I need to get going." I'm an asshole, a piece of shit, but I need space. To think. To figure shit out. Because Sawyer's a fucking game changer, yet she's not even in the game.

"I have to go too," she says, standing. "Abby is over there."

"She can spend the night."

"I'd rather get her now." Her voice is clipped, cold, and that's my fault.

I nod once, and she grabs her clothes, bringing them with her to the bathroom. She's in there for several minutes before she comes out dressed. "Ready."

I should keep my mouth shut because she's giving me an out, but when I look at her sad face, I can't allow myself to do it. So, instead, I step in front of her and pull her into my arms. "I'm sorry," I murmur, burrowing my face into the perfect curve of her neck.

"What's going on?" she asks. "Was it...not good for you?"

I jerk back in shock. "Are you insane? It was...Fuck! Sawyer." I tug on my hair and step back. "I felt it. The chemistry, the sparks. The shit you said when we were talking earlier. I felt it all."

Her mouth curls into a hint of a smile. "I did too," she admits. "So, then, what's wrong?"

"You don't get it!" I bark, turning my back on her, hating myself.

"Then help me get it," she says, entwining her warm, soft hand with mine. She pulls me to the couch and pushes me onto it. Then she climbs into my lap, straddling me. "Talk to me, Hudson."

Her emerald eyes, filled with such raw emotion, are my breaking point. "I was with Clara for over six years, and it was never like that," I tell her, ashamed by my admission. It's one thing to allow myself pleasure, but for our chemistry to override what I had with my wife...Fuck! "It should've been like that," I tell her, dropping my head against her chest. "I was married to her. I loved her. It should've been like it was between us tonight...but it wasn't. So, what does that say about me? About us?"

Sawyer doesn't answer me because she knows there aren't any answers to my questions. I'm feeling guilty because I felt...*feel* more chemistry with her than I did with my wife, and that's not something I can change or fix. Because Clara is gone, buried six feet under the ground, and Sawyer is here, her heart beating, her warm blood coursing through her veins. Clara is gone, and Sawyer is in my arms.

When I glance up, I find her glassy eyes looking at me, silently wishing she could fix me, but what she doesn't realize is that she's already started to. I spent the past five years broken, and in just a few days, Sawyer has begun piecing me back together. I'm not perfect, and the pieces are jagged, and hell, some are still missing, but I feel a thousand times more complete because of her.

My lips meet hers in a slow, sensual caress, silently conveying how much she already means to me. How much I want and need her. She returns the kiss, her fingers dragging through my hair as her center grinds against my pelvis, stoking the flames between us. She reaches down and pulls my dick out of its confines. Stroking it a few times, she pushes her underwear to the side and takes me into her.

Gripping the curves of her hips, I stand and walk us to the wall, pushing her against it. I thrust into her, and the sparks I felt before catch on fire, burning hot between us.

I fuck her fast and deep against the wall until my orgasm slams through me and my hot seed fills her. It's then I realize I've lost my head with this woman. She owns me in every way—mind, body, and soul—and I know I'll do everything in my power to keep her.

When we've both come down from our high, I pull out and watch as my cum drips down the inside of her thigh. Shit! No wonder she felt so good. We didn't use a condom. Her wide eyes meet mine, and I can tell she's just put the pieces together as well, but before she can say a word, I crash my mouth against hers, lifting her into my arms and carrying her to the bathroom so we can shower together.

Once we're both clean, we lie in her bed, me spooning her from behind. "My body fits the curve of yours so perfectly," I whisper into her ear, nestling my face into the crook of her neck. "*We* fit so perfectly."

She nods once, and I worry she's upset because I came in her, so I turn her around to face me. "I'm sorry I came in you." She nods again. "If you're pregnant..."

"No," she says, shaking her head. "Don't go there. I'm going to drive off the island tomorrow and pick up a pill."

For some crazy reason, the thought of her taking something to ensure I can't get her pregnant doesn't sit well with me, but I get it. We just met. She was screwed over by a man before, and I can't blame her for not wanting to take that chance again.

"I'm sorry," I tell her again. "I was caught up in the moment, and I fucked up."

"It's okay," she says, kissing the corner of my mouth before she snuggles into my chest. "I was caught up in the moment just as much as you were."

She kisses my nipple, and I shiver at her touch. I need this woman—not just for this week but forever. I need her words, her touch, her kisses. I need everything that is her. "Sawyer, what if, at the end of your vacation, we didn't—"

But she doesn't let me finish. She lifts her head and kisses me tenderly. "Don't say it," she murmurs against my lips. "We only have a few days left, and I want to spend them with you. And if you say what I think you're going to say, you'll ruin it."

"But—"

"No," she says firmly. "Your life is in New York playing football, and mine is in Tennessee on my family's ranch, and come August, teaching high school."

Her words brook no room for argument, and really, she's not wrong. We live several states apart, and in a few weeks, I'll be signing a contract that ensures New York owns me for at least the next three years. Sawyer deserves more than I can give her. She's young and is just starting her life and deserves to begin her career without having to worry about long-distance phone calls and video chats.

With a heavy heart, I mentally fill a bucket of water and douse the fire blazing between us, watching as the smoke plumes and wishing shit were different, but knowing it's not.

Nine

Hudson

"OH MY GOD," SAWYER MOANS, SITTING UP AND WRAPPING THE blanket around her naked body, save for the tiny thong she has on. "That felt so freaking amazing. I want to do it again… like now."

I laugh as I sit up as well, not bothering with the blanket since I'm in my briefs. "I told you it would be good." I edge off the bed and walk over to the one she's sitting on, caging her in and kissing her softly. "We can do it again if you want, but I was thinking we could also take this back to your room since we still have a few more hours until the kids get out of camp."

Her gaze darts up to the ceiling in thought. "Hmm. Another full-body massage or sex with you. I don't know. The hands on that woman...the way she touched me...was orgasmic." She fans her face, and I pull her off the bed, lifting her over my shoulder.

After we dropped them off at camp this morning, we went to breakfast. While we were eating and deciding what to do with our day, I mentioned getting a couple's massage. I was shocked to learn Sawyer had never gotten a massage, so I insisted we get one. It was a great idea until I was stuck in a room with Sawyer having to watch another woman rub all over her while she moaned in pleasure.

"Hudson," she shrieks as I smack her bare ass and stalk across the room to where our clothes are. "Put me down, you crazy caveman!"

"I'll show you how orgasmic hands can be." I give her cheek another slap, then set her down.

"Fine." She huffs dramatically. "But you better make it worth my while."

For the rest of the afternoon, I use my hands as well as

other parts of my body to get us both off over and over again. When she can't take anymore, and it's almost time to get the kids, she demands to shower alone, saying if we shower together, we'll be late. Since she isn't wrong, I head back to my suite to rinse off and get dressed.

I'm stepping out of the shower when my phone rings with a call from my mother-in-law. Since she rarely calls unless it's important, I answer it.

"Debra, how are you?"

"Hudson." Her tone is cold, and I immediately wonder what's wrong.

"Everything okay?"

"No, everything is not okay," she says, her voice cracking. "It's one thing to sleep around, but it's another to flaunt it for all the world to see."

What the hell is she talking about?

"Debra, you're going to have to explain…"

"It's all over social media. You and that…*woman* buying condoms. You all over her, kissing her and touching her."

I grab my laptop and open it, doing a quick search of my name. Sure enough, several pictures pop up from last night while we were at the store. "I—" I begin, trying to think of how to explain to her what's going on when I don't even really know myself.

But before I can get a single word out, she cuts me off. "I thought you were on a family vacation with your kids."

"I am. I—"

She speaks over me again. "Do you have any idea how humiliating that is for Clara? Do you even care?"

And now, it's my time to talk. "Listen, Debra. I get what you saw looks bad, but I can tell you right now, I've spent the past five years doing nothing but playing football, raising my kids, and grieving over my wife. Until this week, I haven't so much as touched another damn woman," I growl, allowing the pent-up emotions I've been sitting on to finally surface. "I loved Clara with every part of me, but she's gone. And me going to the store to buy condoms with a woman I'm seeing doesn't *embarrass* Clara. It *upsets* you because you're still in denial that she's gone."

"Hudson!" She gasps in shock. "That's out of line!"

"No, it's the truth. It sucks, but she's gone. She's been gone for five damn years, and nothing we do will bring her back. But I'm still here, and..." I drop onto the edge of the bed and sigh. "And I'm lonely," I admit out loud for the first time since I lost my wife. "And Sawyer...she makes me feel a little less alone."

Debra sniffles over the line, and I hate that my truths are hurting her, but it needed to be said because now that I've let Sawyer in, I'm not going to shut everyone else out again. The fact is Sawyer makes me feel a lot less alone. She has me feeling shit I've never felt in my life. I'm happy and living, and it feels like I'm finally moving on, but I don't say any of that to Debra, not wanting to rub salt in her wound.

"It sounds like you're replacing my Clara," she says softly.

"I love my kids, they're my world, but they aren't a proper substitution for adult conversation. Sure, they keep me busy, and they fill my heart with warmth, but they can't fill the void Clara left behind. I'm not replacing her, but for the first time, I am trying to move forward. I'm sorry you had to see those photos, but I'm not sorry I met Sawyer or that I enjoy spending time with her."

Debra is quiet for several beats before she finally speaks. "I understand," she says. "I need to go."

"Okay. I'm here if you need anything."

"Thank you. Please give the kids a kiss for me."

"Will do."

We hang up, and I shoot a message to my publicist, letting her know what's happened so she's not completely blindsided. Then I click on the images, save them, and send them to my phone. I can't even imagine the speculation that's probably all over social media, but I can't stop it now. Let them talk... I'll be busy living.

"I WANT TO SIT NEXT TO SAWYER," PRESLEY ANNOUNCES, plopping in the theater seat to the left of Sawyer. "Me too!" Abby agrees, taking the seat to her right. Both girls snuggle up to her, and she smiles wide, loving the attention.

I glare at the three of them, which only makes them giggle. "Guess you're on your own tonight," Sawyer says with a shrug.

"They only want to sit by you because you hog the popcorn and candy," I point out, making her huff.

"I do not." She pouts.

"You do too," Lucas says, grabbing a bowl of popcorn. "C'mon, Dad, let's sit over here." He walks back one row, so we're seated behind the girls.

"Now we can do this," he whispers conspiratorially when the movie starts, and I press the button to dim the lights.

He picks up a piece of popcorn and flicks it at Presley, hitting her in the back of the head.

She turns around and glares, and he stifles his laugh.

"Do that again, and I'll pour the popcorn on you!" she hisses.

He rolls his eyes, and the second she turns around, he throws a piece at Abby. I should probably stop him, but it's kind of funny to watch. It would be better if we were in a real theater, and they didn't know who was doing it, but the gesture is still hilarious.

"Hey!" Abby swivels around, her nose scrunching up. "That's not nice."

Lucas's face remains stoic. "It wasn't me."

She turns around, and he does it again, this time hitting Sawyer. When she doesn't react, he does it again, clearly wanting her attention. No response. Just as he's about to throw the third piece, all three girls twirl around, and the entire bucket of popcorn comes flying at us. Lucas shrieks in shock, and the girls crack up laughing.

"That's what you get!" Sawyer yells through her laughter.

"Ha!" Lucas says. "Joke's on you 'cause now you have no popcorn." He pops a piece into his mouth, making a show of chomping on it as Sawyer hops over her seat. Before he can grasp what's happening, she snatches the tub out of his hands as the girls cheer her on.

"Hey!" he shouts, jumping up and chasing after her. She runs around the theater, cracking up while he sprints after her.

Then she stops suddenly and turns around, a devilish glint in her eyes. "Don't come any closer."

"Give me my popcorn!" Lucas demands, taking a step toward her.

"If you step another foot toward me, I'll eat it all." She lifts a handful of popcorn to her mouth and chomps down on it.

"You'll choke on it all." Lucas scoffs.

"Fine, then I'll throw it at you."

He crosses his arms over his chest. "Then nobody will have any popcorn."

She shrugs, a tiny smirk playing on her lips.

"Fine." He turns on his heel, making it look like he's giving up, and just when Sawyer thinks she's won, he doubles back and snags the container from her, whooping triumphantly.

"Hey!" she shrieks, going after him as he hightails it away. Abby and Presley join in the chase, giggling. The three of them take him down. The popcorn goes flying as they tickle the hell out of him. As I watch him flop all over the floor like a fish out of water and listen to the girls belly laughing, I think about our life. Are my kids happy? Yes. Do they have a good life? Of course. But the truth is, I've been so busy working, providing that life for them, focused on being their sole provider, that I forgot to actually *live* with them. And that has to change.

The image of the contract sitting on my desk at home pops into my head, and I force myself to swallow down the lump of emotion in my throat. I've spent the past three months with my kids like I do every year after the football season ends. I play from June to January—February if we make the playoffs—so from March to June, I spend my time with my family, going on vacations and relaxing. But for some reason, for the first time in fifteen years, the idea of going back to work has me feeling anxious. And that's definitely something I need to think about.

"Dad!" Lucas shouts. "Help me!"

I cut across the room and lift Sawyer into my arms. "Quit picking on my boy," I joke, smacking her ass as I carry her over to her seat.

"He started it!" she breathes through her laughter.

I set her down and kiss her quickly. "Stay here, woman." I give her a wink, then go back for the other two little devils, who are still tickling Lucas.

Because they're so tiny, I'm able to pick them up with one hand, encircling my arms around their tiny waists. They both giggle while I walk them over to Sawyer, dropping them into their seats.

"Now we have no popcorn," Lucas says like his ass isn't the one who started this.

Sawyer turns around to look at him, a playful smile on

her face. "Maybe if you say please, I'll make us more."

He sighs in defeat. "Will you please make us more popcorn?"

"Well, since you asked so nicely..."

"OH MY GOD!" SAWYER CHOKES OUT A LAUGH, HER HANDS going to her mouth. "Zoom in on that one." I do as she says, zooming in on the photo, and she laughs harder. "Well, at least if they're going to talk, it'll be about the fact that you have a big dick." She points at the box I'm holding that clearly shows the size. "It could be worse," she says through a laugh. "You could have a small pecker, and everyone would know."

I chuck my phone onto the bed and drop on top of her, tickling the hell out of her. When she screams, I cover her mouth with my own so she doesn't wake the kids. They've fallen asleep watching a movie, and Sawyer and I are in my room, messing around on my bed.

"I should probably head back to my room," she says when I break the kiss. "I feel like we've taken over yours."

"Not happening." I kiss my way down her neck.

"I feel bad that I've hardly been in my own room," she says, though the breathlessness in her voice tells me otherwise. "My sister paid for it, and I've spent the past three nights with you."

Just as I'm about to make my argument, my phone rings out through the room. I lift it to see who it is, and when I see it's my mom, I groan. She no doubt saw the pictures on social media and wants all the details. When it stops and then starts again, I know I have to answer it.

"It's my mom."

I climb off Sawyer and sit against the headboard so I can answer it. She nods, sitting up and fixing her clothes. She's about to get off the bed, but before she can, I pull her between my legs. "You're not going anywhere," I murmur against her lips before I answer the call. Sawyer snuggles into me, her head going to my chest as she stretches her legs out.

"Hey, Mom."

"Hudson James Matthews, I haven't heard from you in several days. You know better than that. I thought you loved me."

I chuckle at her chiding, knowing she's only partly messing with me. We do talk several times a week, but she knew with me being away with the kids, I wouldn't call her as often.

"How are you and dad?" I ask, ignoring her accusation.

"I'd be better if I heard from my only child once in a while. How are my grandbabies? Are they having a good time?"

"They're good. Loving camp and the beach and the pool.

"That's good. That's good. And how are you?"

"Mom, how about you ask the question you really want to ask?" I say with a laugh.

She huffs over the line. "Fine, since you're going to make me...Who is that adorable woman in the picture with you?"

I know Sawyer can hear our conversation when her entire body stiffens at my mom's words. I lean over and kiss the crown of her hair. "She's a friend."

Mom huffs harder. "A friend with benefits?"

I chuckle. "How do you even know what that is?"

"I watch cable."

Sawyer snorts out a laugh, then covers her face with her

hands.

"You haven't been seen with a single woman since..." She doesn't need to finish her sentence for me to know where she's going.

"I know. I met Sawyer here. She and her daughter are staying at the same resort as us." Sawyer slides down, so her head is in my lap, and she glances up at me. Her green eyes remind me of a football field. Every time I step foot on the turf, it's a fresh start. A new game. A new opportunity. Everything else just fades away.

My mom is talking on the other end, but all I can focus on is the woman in front of me. Her bright eyes. Plump lips. The way she smiles up at me in contentment. It took months before I knew I was in love with my wife, yet as I glance down at Sawyer, I know, without a shadow of a doubt, she's my fresh start.

"Mom, I need to call you back."

"What? Is everything okay?"

"Yeah, we'll talk soon. I promise."

We hang up and I throw my phone onto the bedside table, then pull out from under Sawyer, so I'm on top of her, my arms caging her in. "I don't want this to end," I tell her, putting it all on the line. "Don't leave on Saturday. Stay here with me, please. We can figure it out. I've never felt like this before."

She gasps at my admission and then immediately shakes her head. "Don't do this, Hudson," she begs, pushing me back. "Don't ruin the last few days we have together."

She sits up and climbs off the bed, crossing her arms over her chest. "You're thinking with your dick, not your head."

"No, I'm thinking with my heart."

She sucks in a harsh breath. "Stop it." She walks to the door, but I catch her before she makes it out.

"Stop, what? Admitting that these past few days have been amazing. That I came on vacation to escape my life and found a woman I want to spend my life with."

"Hudson!" she barks. "Enough. Stop saying this shit. We've been having fun, but that's all it is...fun. Nothing more. I told you I don't date famous people and I meant it. Right now, you're caught up in the moment, but the second you're back at work, traveling from city to city, doing what you love, you'll forget all about me...about us."

Before I can refute her statement, tell her she's wrong, that I could never forget her, she turns her back on me and stalks through the suite, straight to the theater room. When she gets in there, she scoops her daughter up into her arms.

"Don't go, please."

"I have to," she whisper-yells. "I need some space...We need some space. You're talking crazy and I...I...I just need to go."

I want to argue with her, but Abby's eyes open, landing on me, so I close my mouth, nodding. With her daughter in her arms, she leaves in a rush. I hate that she's walking through the dark, but by the time I would get Joanie over here, she'd already be at her room. So, instead, I send her a text asking her to please let me know she made it back okay. A few minutes later a text comes through confirming she's fine.

I consider texting her back, but what would I say? She made it clear how she feels about dating someone whose job requires him to travel and be in the spotlight. I could argue that I'm nothing like her ex, but she's already lumped me into the same category by default. So, instead, I decide to give her the space she asked for, while I figure out how to convince her that what we have is worth pursuing.

Ten

Sawyer

"BUT THE SPLASH PAD IS FOR BABIES." ABBY POUTS. "WHY CAN'T I go to camp with Presley? It's so unfair." She stomps her foot and glares my way, making me feel like shit. Normally, I wouldn't put up with that kind of attitude from my daughter, but since it's my fault she's behaving this way, it makes it hard to reprimand her.

When she woke up this morning, excited to go to camp and see Presley, I insisted we instead spend the day with just the two of us. After the shit Hudson flung at me last night, there was no way I was going anywhere he might be. Yes, I'm aware I'm behaving like a scaredy-cat child, but it is what it is. Because everything Hudson said to me, I feel it too. But he's not part of my plans and I'm not a part of his. He lives in New York, while I live in Tennessee. He plays professional football and I'm about to start my first job teaching high school. Until now, our vast age difference didn't matter. But when you take that fact and add it to everything else, it's clear we're at two different points in our lives and thinking we can continue what we have here would be setting ourselves up for heartbreak.

I meant what I said when we first met. I'm not looking to date anyone famous again. He might not be a musician like my ex, but he still falls in the same category of constant travel, women fawning all over him, and his face and business constantly in the public eye. All things I can't and don't want to compete with. I'm a small-town girl with zero desire to live in the city.

"Presley! Lucas!" Abby yells. I'm about to tell her it's not happening, when Hudson and his two kids appear in front of us, and I realize she wasn't yelling for them but calling them over.

"Crazy running into you guys here," Hudson says, winking at me like I didn't run out of his room last night like my ass was on fire.

"No, it's not," Lucas says. "You said we were going to find them since Abby didn't go to camp."

I glare daggers at Hudson, who doesn't appear even a little bit embarrassed over his son calling him out.

"True," he says, dropping an arm around my shoulders. "We have an exciting day planned and we all agreed it wouldn't be the same without you two."

Presley and Lucas both nod in agreement.

"Hudson," I grind out. "Can I talk to you for a minute?"

"No time," he says. "Now, who's ready for a fun-filled day?"

All three kids cheer in unison excitedly, and I know, unless I want an extremely unhappy child, I'm going to have to go along with this.

Twenty minutes later, we're standing with golf clubs and balls in our hands at the first hole of a mini golf course. Lucas offers to go first, hitting the ball with brute force and sending it flying down the straightaway with perfect precision.

"Have you ever played golf before?" I ask, seriously impressed. I don't know much about the sport, but in one hit, he almost made it into the hole. It usually takes me like fifteen times.

"Yep," he says with pride in his voice. "Since I was three."

"Really?" I laugh, imagining Abby at three years old playing an old man's sport. "I thought kids played soccer."

Hudson shakes his head. "I tried that, but it wasn't happening. Took him golfing with me one day and he loved it, so I signed him up for lessons."

"I do gymnastics," Presley says. "Watch this!" She drops her club on the ground and jumps into a cartwheel. When she lands, she raises her arms and says, "Ta da!"

"Wow!" Abby breathes. "I want to do that too!"

"I can show you," Presley says, taking her and forgetting about the golf game.

The girls go to the side, doing cartwheels and giggling when they clash into each other while Lucas, Hudson, and I continue the golf game. The girls occasionally join in, but for the most part they play around, doing cartwheels and somersaults on the soft turf. When we finish, Lucas is declared the winner, and the girls give him a fake crown.

"Can we go to the pool?" Presley asks as we walk to the car.

"Yeah!" Abby agrees. "But no splash pad." She side-eyes me, making me roll my eyes.

"Sure," Hudson agrees easily. "But how about we go eat first? They're doing a movie night in the pool, so we can go to that after dinner."

"Yay!" The kids cheer, on cloud nine.

"I spoke to Joanie," Hudson says, pulling me into his side. "She's going to watch the kids tomorrow during the day and at night. I want to take you out."

"Hudson," I groan.

"Please," he says, stopping and looking at me. "I heard you, I get it, but tomorrow is our last day together before you leave. Let me spend it with you. The kids will have fun together at camp, and Joanie will take them bowling in the afternoon."

"There's a bowling alley at the hotel?"

"No, but there's one in my suite next to the theater." He

shrugs, and I laugh at how different our lives and worlds are. I was just excited my room had a spa tub.

"Please," he says again, his blue eyes pleading.

"Okay," I give in. "But I need to go to my room tonight so I can start packing and get things ready. We leave at seven to catch our flight."

"WE'RE GOING ON THIS BOAT?" I POINT AT THE MONSTROSITY that's nothing like the last one we went on. This one is like the Daddy boat, and the other one was the baby.

"It's technically a yacht, but yeah."

"Can you drive this thing?"

Hudson laughs. "Probably, but I'm not going to. There's a driver, so I can spend my time with you instead of having to focus on driving."

We board the yacht, and Hudson shows me around. It has two levels and is more like a small apartment than a boat—the thing even has a bedroom with a king-sized bed!

Once we're situated, the boat leaves the marina, and

Hudson guides me to the huge lounge area in the front. I take off my cover-up, and Hudson applies sunscreen to my back. Then I return the favor, rubbing the lotion all over his muscular back and shoulders. After we're both covered, we lie on the fluffy, comfortable cushions.

My eyes close, relishing in the quiet and calm of the water lapping around us. I should probably feel guilty for being on this gorgeous yacht while Abby is at camp, but she couldn't wait to go this morning, and she loves spending time with Presley and Lucas. I can't even imagine how devastated she's going to be tomorrow night when we have to say goodbye. She doesn't make friends easily, and she let them into her heart so effortlessly. My heart constricts behind my rib cage. The truth is, she isn't the only one who's going to miss them. I've grown to care about both of them during our short time together.

"What has you frowning?" Hudson asks. I open my eyes and find him on his side, facing me. He pulls me closer to him, his strong hand landing on my thigh. My thoughts go to last night, his admissions. Being with him would be as easy as breathing... if we lived in the same area, had a similar lifestyle.

"I was thinking about how much Abby is going to miss Presley and Lucas...And how much I'm going to miss them... and you."

Hudson nods. "It doesn't have to be like this..."

"And what—we agree to do the long-distance thing? I go home and teach while you travel all over playing football. We'll try to see each other on a weekend you aren't playing or during a holiday break. We'll miss each other, but the stress of trying to make it work will tear us apart. It will confuse the kids, and in the end, we won't be able to make it work."

I roll onto my stomach and prop myself up on his chest, so we're face-to-face. "We're the perfect case of wrong timing. I would rather walk away Saturday morning on good terms, feeling blessed to have met you. When I look back at this trip, at the pictures and memories, I want to remember the fun times we had, and I don't want them being soiled by our attempt to make something more out of this."

Hudson shakes his head. "I don't like this. I don't want to agree to that."

"I don't either," I admit, "but it's what's for the best.

Meeting you and your kids was such an unexpected surprise, one I'll never forget. But we're on two different paths that aren't destined to cross."

"What if they do?" Hudson asks. "What if our paths one day cross?"

"Then I guess we'll see where they take us."

"NO PEEKING," HUDSON SAYS, GUIDING ME THROUGH THE SAND.

"Where are we going?"

"You'll see..."

Tomorrow morning, Abby and I are leaving at six, so the kids are spending their last night together with Joanie watching them while Hudson takes me on our last date before we part ways. I told him I think it's best if Abby and I spend the night in our room, so it's easier to get ready to go. It'll be early, and we don't want to disturb everyone. It will also be a lot harder to say goodbye tomorrow morning instead of tonight. Thankfully, he agreed.

"If you walk me out into the ocean, I'm going to kill you."

Hudson chuckles but doesn't say anything. A minute later, we stop, and he steps behind me, encircling his arms around me. "Okay, you can remove your blindfold."

It takes a few seconds for my eyes to adjust in the dark, but once I do, I'm completely taken aback by the sight in front of me. There's a large private cabana situated in the sand with blankets and pillows covering the ground. Tiki torches surround the area to add a hint of light in the darkness.

Hudson turns me around so I can see the other half of his surprise. An oversized blowup screen is several feet away with a stilled image projecting against it.

"We're watching a movie out here?" I breathe in awe of what he's done.

"Yep. It's just the two of us. I spoke to the owner of the property, and since it's private, no one will bother us."

I glance around and realize that while we're on the beach, the hotel isn't in the background. Instead, it's only overgrown shrubbery and the peaks of a couple of houses. We must've walked farther than I thought.

"This is amazing," I tell Hudson, wrapping my arms around his neck and pressing my lips to his for a chaste kiss.

"What movie are we watching?"

He takes my hand and walks us over to the cabana. We kick off our flip-flops and drop onto the feather-like pillows and blankets. When he clicks play and the title of the movie appears, I squeal in excitement.

"Are you freaking serious? This movie isn't even out yet!" I've been reading the book again in preparation for the movie that comes out next month, and I told Hudson as much one night when he asked what I was reading on my e-reader.

"I got the hookup," he says with a shrug. "I called in a favor and had it overnighted. I also got all your favorites." He points at the small table filled with popcorn and candy and drinks. "I figured if I only have one last night with you, I better make it count."

The fact that he did all this isn't what makes my heart flutter in my chest. It's that he paid attention to what I was saying, to what I'm interested in, to what I like. One day, when he meets the right woman at the right time, he's going to make an amazing husband. I have no doubt he already was one to Clara. And it breaks my heart that he has to start all over again. He did everything right, yet he still ended up heartbroken.

We snuggle up together with my head on his chest, my arm thrown over his torso, and our legs entwined in each other. Hudson presses play, and the movie begins, the sound coming in close to us. There must be surround sound in the cabana somewhere.

While we watch the movie, Hudson runs his fingers along my flesh, down my arm, and across my back. He doesn't take it any further, but the entire time, even when we are eating the snacks and sipping on the drinks, he's touching me in some way. The movie is about a couple who love each other but—ironically, similarly to us—the timing is off. This is the final movie in the series, and instead of getting their happily ever after right away, they go their separate ways. When this happens, tears flow down my cheeks. I knew it was coming since I've read the books twice, but it's hard to watch, especially since I can relate. As the story continues, they meet other people, date, fall in love, live their lives, but you can see it in their eyes—they miss each other.

Finally, their lives bring them back together, and although it isn't easy, they find their happy ending. When the credits roll at the end, I sit up, wiping the liquid from my face.

"That's us," Hudson says, his glassy eyes meeting mine. "We're right for each other in every way, but our circumstances won't allow us to be together."

"I know," I rasp, fresh tears filling my eyes.

"They found their way," he says, taking my face in his hands. "We can find a way. Please, Sawyer. Don't let this be the end of us."

"I can't do it," I cry out. "Abby's dad traveled for work, and it ended with him cheating on me and forgetting we exist. He chose a life on the road over us. I can't do it again. I'm sorry. I'm sorry..." I shake my head, sobs wracking my body. I hate that it has to be this way, but I don't know what else to do.

"Please, Sawyer," he begs. "Don't punish us for the shit your ex did."

He tucks a stray hair behind my ear and gives me a kiss. His lips are strong yet soft, and I sigh into the kiss, loving how good he tastes. "Please, Sawyer. Don't push me away because you've been hurt. I'm not him. Give me a chance to prove it to you."

"And what if it doesn't work out?" I ask, shocked I'm even considering this.

"You can't live like that, always wondering what if. That'll drive you insane and stop you from loving." His words come out melancholy, and I know he's referring to his past, to his late wife, and how he lost her far too soon. And that thought has me pushing past my insecurities, my fears, because if Hudson can experience a loss that devastating and still be willing to take a chance on love, then I can too.

"Okay," I murmur. "I'll give us a chance."

"You will?" he asks in shock.

"Yeah. I don't know how the hell it's going to work, but I'm willing to take the risk...on you...on us."

"Fuck, yes. I promise, you won't regret it." His lips connect with mine for a desperate, bruising kiss, and I wrap myself around him, needing to feel our bodies against each other.

Our clothes come off, and Hudson lays me out on the pillow bed, devouring my mouth before he moves down my body to ravish every inch of me. He nips and sucks on my flesh. I pull his face up to meet mine and crash my lips against his. His fingers glide between my legs, and he thrusts a couple inside me, fucking me deep and hard. His thumb massages my clit, and he breaks our kiss, peppering tender kisses along my jaw, my cheeks, my chin, my neck. It's as though Hudson is determined to learn every inch of my body before we part ways.

His lips clamp down on my nipple, and I shudder as an orgasm rips through me, waves of pleasure rolling through me.

"Fuck, I love the way your pussy tightens around my fingers when you come," Hudson says as he pulls them out and makes a show of licking my release from them.

"Get inside me," I groan, reaching forward and taking his dick in my hand. I pull him over me and stroke him up and down, getting him hard. "Do you have a...?"

"Yeah." Blindly reaching for his shorts, he pulls a square foil packet out and hands it to me so I can put it on him.

Once he's covered, his hands land on either side of my head, and he enters me in one fluid motion, our bodies becoming one. Hudson makes love to me slowly, languorously, his heated gaze staying locked on mine. As he pushes in and out of me, filling me deliciously, my heart gallops in my chest, my need for him growing like a tree's roots latching on and spreading. I'm suddenly overcome with raw emotions as I wonder how I'm ever going to walk away from him come tomorrow. Even though we've both decided to take the risk and see where things go, I can't help the fear that this could be our last time together. No matter how much we want us to work off this island, the odds are stacked against us.

Hudson makes sure I've come again before he pulls me onto his lap to straddle him and thrusts hard and deep from under me, finding his own release. With him still inside me, our bodies pulsing with adrenaline, he cups my face and brushes his lips against mine.

"I love you, Sawyer," he whispers against my lips. "I know you're afraid of being hurt, but I promise your heart is safe with me."

"I love you too," I tell him honestly as I store his confession of love and promise deep in my heart, so later, when I'm back home and alone and cold, I can use them as a blanket, wrapping them around me to keep myself warm.

Eleven

Hudson

I miss you.

I wish you were here.

Are you ignoring me?

Sawyer...

I STARE AT MY PHONE, WILLING THE BUBBLES TO APPEAR. IT'S been two weeks since we returned home from our vacation and three since I've seen Sawyer. After she agreed to give us a chance and we made love, I asked her to stay an extra week with us. I offered to move them to my suite, and when she said we needed to take things slow and not jump right in like that with the kids, I told her I would pay for another room and to have her flight changed. She smiled, told me again that she loved me, and then said we need to take things slow. She needed to get home for the orientation she's required to attend at work, and we would see each other soon.

I start training camp next week, and the closer it creeps toward the date, the more anxious I get. The kids and I have been busy, spending our time in the pool and going on the boat. Both their grandparents—Clara's mom and my parents—have visited, but what I want is to see Sawyer.

Once training begins, my life becomes crazy. I asked her to come visit before that, but she said she wasn't sure if she could. As I pace back and forth in my office, wearing a hole into the floor, I wonder if maybe she was right. If I'm pushing so hard to see her because I know I'm going to be busy once the season starts, how the hell are we going to find time to see each other during the season?

It would be a lot easier if she lived closer, and selfishly,

I was thinking maybe if I could get her and Abby to visit so she could see where I live isn't so bad, I could somehow convince her to move here. Then we could see each other a hell of a lot more.

My phone buzzes in my hand, and I open the message, hoping it's Sawyer, but it's just Deacon, a good friend of mine from the Bluebirds, confirming the time and place we're meeting for dinner tonight. He and his new fiancée are celebrating their engagement and invited a few of us to join them. I'd rather hang out at home and text and video chat with Sawyer, but I promised I would go.

As I'm texting him back that I'll see them later, a shadow in my doorway has me looking up. I'm expecting it to be Joanie, since she arrived a little bit ago to keep an eye on the kids so I can meet a couple of my teammates—and friends— at the gym to get a workout in, so I'm shocked when I find Sawyer leaning against the doorframe.

"She never texted you back, did she?" she asks, nodding toward my phone in my hand.

"No, she didn't. But I think I can forgive her since she's here." I cut across the room and pull her into my arms, kissing the shit out of her. "You're here."

"I am." She smiles up at me. "Joanie let me in."

"How long are you here for?" I ask, then hold my breath, hoping she'll say forever.

"The weekend. Next week, I have a couple of days of required training for work. It's crazy that summer will be over in a few short weeks. Teachers go back two weeks before the students."

My heart sinks. Two days. That's all I have with her, and then we'll both be busy. I shake the negativity from my thoughts. We'll figure it out. Right now, she's here, and I don't want to taint our time together.

"Is Abby here?"

"She is." She looks at me, a little worried. "I couldn't leave her with my—"

"Stop. I'm glad she's here. The kids will be excited to see her. Fuck." I lift her into my arms again and devour her mouth. "I can't believe you're actually here."

My phone goes off, reminding me I left my friend hanging. "Let me text Deacon and cancel for tonight, and then I'm all yours." I also need to text Clay and let him know

I won't be meeting him and the other guys at the gym. *Fuck working out, my woman's here.*

"Wait," she says, placing her hand over the phone. "You had plans tonight? I don't want to intrude. I should've told you I was coming..."

"Hey, stop." I cup her face. "This is the best damn surprise. I'm so happy you're here." Then it hits me. "Come with me tonight."

Her nose scrunches up. "Where?"

"Dinner with some friends. Deacon and his fiancée, Katie, are celebrating their engagement. Joanie is watching the kids. We can go eat, dance, then come home, and I can relearn every inch of your body all night." I fist her hair and tilt her head to kiss the side of her neck. She smells like lavender, and my dick is instantly hard.

"Fuck dinner, let's go straight to the bed." I make a show out of eating her neck, and she throws her head back with a laugh.

"No way. We are not spending our time in bed. You promised to show me around if I came, and here I am. I want to see everything."

Since I'm not going to the gym anymore, Joanie says she has some errands to run and will be back later. I show Sawyer around the house, and while we're outside by the pool, Presley wakes up from her nap. The kids beg to go swimming, so we spend the afternoon in the pool.

Joanie returns in the late afternoon, taking over with the kids so Sawyer and I can get ready for tonight. When she steps out of the bathroom in a pair of skintight ripped jeans, a top that shows off her perfect round breasts, and fuck me heels, I reconsider going anywhere but to bed.

"No." She raises her finger and wags it back and forth.

"What?"

"I see that look in your eye. We're going out."

"Fine." I sigh. My hands go straight to her ass, and I tug her toward me. "You look gorgeous."

"Same for you." She runs her fingers along the collar of my button-down shirt. "I've missed you." She kisses the corner of my mouth, and I turn my face to deepen the kiss. We're still kissing when my phone goes off, letting me know our car is here.

"You don't drive?" she asks.

"Not in the city. And definitely not if I plan to drink."

After saying bye to the kids, who are too busy planning their movie night with Joanie to care, we take off toward the city. It's Friday night, and the traffic sucks, but it doesn't bother me because I get to spend the drive making out with Sawyer.

When we arrive, the driver already knows to pick us up when I text him, so we get out and head to the hostess stand. We're at Olive's, a huge celebrity spot, so I'm not surprised when paparazzi are outside taking pictures. With Sawyer on my arm, I'm sure the rumor mill will be buzzing, so before they can get to it, I snap a selfie of us and post it on my social media with a caption that makes it clear she's someone important.

"Did you tag me in your post?" she asks, her eyes wide.

"Yeah. I had to make it clear..."

"What?"

I step into her space and wrap my arms around her waist, then press my mouth to hers. "That you're my woman," I murmur against her lips.

Dinner is fun. For the first time in a long ass time, I'm

not a fifth wheel. Everyone loves Sawyer, and we spend the night eating, drinking, and dancing. She might not be a city girl, but she fits in like a perfect-sized glove.

When we get home, the kids are already asleep. I spend the night rememorizing every part of her until we both pass out, our bodies tangled in each other.

I wake to an empty bed, and for a second, I worry maybe I was dreaming that she was here. But then I hear the sound of her melodic laughter.

After taking a quick shower and getting dressed, I head downstairs and find Sawyer and the three kids dancing to some pop song while they help her make breakfast. The sight in front of me has me stopping in my place and pulling out my phone to take a couple of pictures. So I can remember what she looks like in my kitchen, carefree and laughing. Until I can somehow convince her to stay forever.

"There you are," she says when she notices me here. "You're just in time. We made chocolate chip pancakes with peanut butter."

"Yeah!" Abby adds. "It's our favorite."

The kids all help set the table while Sawyer puts the

food out, and I pour the drinks. If you were watching us from the outside, you would think we've been a family for years, instead of this being the first time we've ever had breakfast—the five of us at home. But that's just the way it is with us. Everything has come so fucking naturally from the beginning.

The weekend flies by way too damn quickly, and before I know it, I'm kissing Sawyer goodbye at the airport while Presley hugs Abby. Everyone is sad as hell to say goodbye, but there's nothing I can do. I told Sawyer I would figure this out, but the truth is, I'm not sure how to go about that. The thought scares the shit out of me because what if Sawyer was right? What if our timing is off, and by stringing us along, all I'm doing is hurting everyone in the process?

No, I tell myself. *That's not going to happen.* I'm going to figure this shit out. Just like in football, I need to come up with a game plan. I've won five damn Super Bowls. Surely, I can figure out how to get Sawyer and me in the same damn state for longer than a few days.

Twelve

Hudson

"GET IT! GET IT!"

"We're not a moving target on this!"

"C'mon, Matthews, get it together!"

"Go... Go... Go!"

I make pass after pass, but more often than not, I'm missing my mark. My coaches yell, and my teammates grumble, but I'm struggling. It shouldn't be like this. We're a well-oiled machine with five rings as proof of what we're capable of. But I'm failing my team because my head's not in it.

It's been three weeks since I had to say goodbye to Sawyer at the airport. Training camp has started, and I can't focus. I text her every day, asking how her day was and what she was up to. She's busy preparing for the upcoming school year and for Abby's birthday party. At first, she would respond with long, detailed messages. But with each passing day, her responses get shorter and farther apart. I can feel her slipping through my fingers, and I don't know what the hell to do about it.

"Dammit, Matthews. What the hell is going on?" Coach barks, frustration seeping through every word. "We're done for the day." The disappointed, confused look he gives me has my heart plummeting into my stomach. These men are like family, and I'm failing them. My head and heart aren't in it, and it's not fair to them. I need to get it together.

I rip my helmet off and head to the showers with the other guys. I can feel their eyes on me, wanting to know what's going on, but they don't ask. They trust me. They've trusted me for years.

The second I'm outside, I pull my phone out of my bag and find several missed calls from Joanie. My heart stutters in fear when I worry something happened to one of my kids.

"Hudson, thank you for calling me back. I normally wouldn't bother you while you're at work, but—"

"It's fine. Is everything okay?" I ask, worried.

"No, it's not. Presley and Lucas got into an argument with a boy at camp. Lucas hit him, and I was asked to pick them up. He's been suspended for a week."

My thoughts go back to the last boy Lucas hit...in defense of Abby. "Did he say what happened?"

"No, neither of them will speak. They both went to their rooms when we got home, and they won't come out or say a word."

"All right, I'm on my way home."

"Okay, umm...Hudson..."

"Yeah?"

"I don't mean to overstep, but this is the third time in two weeks they've gotten in trouble. I don't know what's going on, but it's not like them. And their attitudes...It's like they're mad at the world."

"You're not overstepping. I know. They're not mad at the world...They're mad at me." They've made it clear on several occasions. The first when we had to say goodbye to Abby and Sawyer at the airport. Lucas was quiet about it at first until Presley started crying. Then he blamed me for upsetting her. I tried to explain it's not my fault, and it was because we live in two different states, but he argued that I'm rich and can have whatever I want. I didn't bother to explain that's not how life works. He was an upset eight-year-old lashing out and wanted me to make it right. My heart cracked.

The next time they got mad was when we received Abby's birthday invitation in the mail, and I told them we couldn't go because I have to work. Lucas proceeded to scream at me and let me know that my job is ruining their lives, while Presley cried that Abby is going to forget her and they'll never be friends again. My heart broke.

Then I sent them to camp. A camp Lucas has gone to every year. It's run by the school, so Lucas usually loves it because he gets to hang out with his friends. This is Presley's first time since she's starting kindergarten. They both complained the entire way there and begged me to let them stay home. They asked to go away again with me, saying we had so much fun and why don't I want to be with them. I explained I have to work for a living, and my job requires me to go back now. Lucas looked me dead in the eyes and told me he hates my job and hates me. And my heart shattered.

I arrive to a quiet home, and Joanie greets me in the foyer with a sad smile. "Lucas is awake, sulking, and Presley is asleep. I tried to pry it out of him what happened, but he's not talking."

"Thanks." I step into the kitchen and open the fridge to grab a bottle of water. As I close it, the bright pink invitation, dated for this weekend, catches my eye, and I make a last-minute decision, consequences be damned. "We're going out of town for a few days, so I won't need you. We should be home Monday, but I'll text and let you know for sure."

She smiles knowingly. "Sounds good."

Once she's gone, and I've showered and gotten dressed, I head to Lucas's room to speak with him first while Presley is asleep. He's curled up in his reading chair with a book in his hands. Joanie must've taken his electronics away until I got home.

"Hey."

He glances up and eyes me quickly, muttering, "Hey,"

back before he returns his attention to his book.

I step into his room and sit on the ottoman in front of him. "We need to talk." He sighs but gives me the respect of closing his book and looking at me. "What happened at camp? And don't shrug, please," I warn, knowing he'll first resort to that.

His hazel eyes, filled with emotion, hit me hard. While he looks like me—aside from having her hazel eyes—his personality is all her. He loves hard and protects those he loves even harder.

"Brecken told Presley that his mom said Presley killed our mom. I warned him to shut up, but he wouldn't listen. He said no mom would want to die, so we'll never have another mom."

One of the good and bad things about living in the same area your entire life is that you grow up with the same kids, which means everyone knows everyone. Brecken's mom, Sandra, and Clara were acquaintances at best. They were in the same mom's group and later enrolled the kids in the same private school before Clara passed away. Sandra was bitter because her husband had cheated and liked to point out no man could be faithful. Unsure where to go when Clara passed away, I kept my kids in the private school all the rich clique parents in our neighborhood had their kids enrolled in.

"Brecken's mom is wrong," I tell my son. "Your mom died due to a rare condition, but it wasn't because of Presley."

"I know," he says softly, "but umm..." He glances down, and I lift his chin to look at me.

"But what?"

"Presley and I were kind of hoping Sawyer would be our new mom, but then she left because you have to work. She was really nice, and she's Abby's mom, so she knows how to be a mom."

A lump of emotion clogs my throat, and I pull him into my arms, momentarily hating God and science and fate. "Sawyer is really nice, and she is a great mom, but she didn't leave because I have to work. She left because she lives in a different state, and she has to work there."

"I hate work," he mutters into my chest.

"Daddy," Presley grumbles in the doorway, rubbing the sleep out of her eyes.

"Come here, sweetie." I open my arms out for her, and

she joins Lucas and me in a family hug. "Your brother told me what Brecken said…"

I pull back so I can look her in the eyes. "You are not the reason your mom is gone. She loved you and Lucas more than anything in this world, but she got sick and had to go to heaven."

"Why did I never meet her?"

"What? You did." I walk over to the bedside table and grab the picture frame. "This is you when you were a baby with your mom."

"I know," Presley says, "but I don't remember that."

My heart clenches in my chest. No matter what I do, I'll never be able to make it to where Presley remembers anything about her mom.

"I know, sweetie, but if you want to know anything about her, I can tell you. She loved the color pink, just like you do, and she had the same hazel eyes as you and Lucas. She loved breakfast for dinner, and she hated football, just like you do."

Presley giggles. "Football is boring."

"It is not." I tickle her playfully, making her cry out.

"Is so!" she squeals.

"Abby's birthday is Saturday. How would you feel about taking a trip to Tennessee and going to her party?"

Both kids perk up.

"Really?" Presley asks.

"Really. We can leave tomorrow morning and come back Monday."

"Yay!" both kids cheer.

I leave them to pick out some clothes for the trip even though I'm sure I'll have to check them all before packing them and start making arrangements. I find a flight leaving New York early tomorrow morning. I book a rental SUV and then book a hotel about twenty minutes from Sawyer's family's farm. Then I remember I never told her we're coming... I should probably tell her, but I decide to keep it a secret, the same way she did when she visited me. It'll be more fun that way. And... she won't be able to tell me not to come.

WE GET OFF THE PLANE AND, AFTER GRABBING OUR RENTAL, stop at the store on the way to the party to pick up a gift for Abby. The kids insist on picking it out. Presley goes with a princess splash pad, and Lucas insists on water guns—at least they're pink.

Since the party is starting soon, we head straight there. As we drive through the town, the kids point out how different it is. Presley mentions that there are a lot of trees and green and people in cowboy boots with cowboy hats. Lucas points out the people riding horses along the sidewalk and the lack of traffic. While we don't live directly in the city, it's all they've ever known. Even our version of suburbia has more concrete and traffic than Sawyer's town.

I take in the town as we drive down what appears to be their main street. It looks like the shit you see in those small-town movies where everyone knows everyone. A sign hanging on the street corner announces a fall festival next month, and I laugh to myself—totally something you would see in a movie. I can't deny how down-to-earth it all feels, though. It's as if nobody is in a rush. No cars are honking or speeding. Kids who appear to be my son's age are riding bikes and scooters along the sidewalks. I can't imagine letting him go anywhere outside of our yard without me. Even in our gated community, the traffic is too bad for him to just up and leave on his own.

When we arrive at the farm, there are several pink and white balloons at the entrance, along with an iron sign that reads Addison Farms.

"Are we here?" Presley asks, bouncing in her booster seat with her face pressed up against the window.

"I think so." My nerves kick in, wondering if I made a mistake showing up unannounced when nothing has changed. *Because you're in love with her, and something needs to change...*

We drive down a long, winding dirt road until we reach a decent size two-story farmhouse. There are a couple of vehicles outside, but we're clearly early, which is probably a good thing since they'll be in a bit of a shock to see us here.

Before we can get out, the front door swings open and Abby comes running out in her pink princess dress with a crown on top of her head to greet whichever guest has arrived. The second we step out of the vehicle, and she sees it's us, she stops in her place for a moment, then runs at full speed straight to Presley, who's running as well and meets her halfway. The girls squeal in delight with their arms around each other, jumping up and down.

"How'd you get here?" Abby asks with a smile on her face.

"I rode on a big plane and then drove in the car," Presley answers.

I chuckle at her literal answer, but my laughter comes to a screeching halt the second I spot the gorgeous woman standing just outside the front door on the porch. She's dressed in a pair of cutoffs that showcase her sexy, tanned legs and a yellow flowy top that rides up high on her belly, exposing her toned stomach. Her gorgeous green eyes meet mine with a look of confusion marring her features.

"Hey, Sawyer," Lucas says, his voice bordering on timid and nervous. My thoughts go back to our unfinished conversation yesterday, and I hold my breath, praying Sawyer doesn't take her shock out on him. Of course, she proves to be amazing, when her gaze goes to him and her face brightens like the fucking sun.

"Lucas! I can't believe you're here!" She walks down the steps and over to him, enveloping him in a hug. He wraps his arms around her, and my heart both breaks and gets pieced together at the same time. They part, and she hugs Presley next. "I'm so happy to see you guys."

"They came for my birthday," Abby says. "You said they weren't coming. Why did you lie?"

"She didn't lie," I jump in before Sawyer can get a word in. "We weren't supposed to come. I was supposed to work, but I took a few days off and wanted to surprise you guys."

"Yay!" Abby cheers. "Come here, Presley. Come see my cake." She takes her hand and is about to run in, but then stops. "Lucas, you can come too. It's pink, but my grandma made chocolate cake under it."

"That's cool," Lucas says, following them inside and leaving Sawyer and me alone.

"You're here," Sawyer breathes, turning her attention to me.

"I'm here."

Thirteen

Sawyer

HE'S HERE. IN MY STATE, IN MY TOWN, AT MY HOUSE. WITH HIS kids. When I hugged Lucas and Presley, my heart swelled in my chest. Since we've returned home from vacation, it's felt like a piece of me was missing. It's the reason I made the last-second decision to visit them, and it's also why I've been distancing myself from him recently. Every time we're together, I feel whole, complete, like everything is right in the world, and then our time together ends, and we have to part ways, and it feels as though Hudson and his children take a vital piece of me with them.

"I wanted to surprise you," he says, giving me the same reason I gave him when I showed up unannounced. The difference is, he had asked me that morning to come see him. Jokingly, I told him I would hop on a plane right away. And then, without second-guessing myself, I did something crazy and got online and booked Abby and me a flight on my credit card, showing up at his house a few hours later.

He, on the other hand, didn't tell me because I've been pushing him away the past week. The more I miss him, the more my heart hurts, and the more I push him away because I don't know what else to do. We're at an impasse, and neither of us can make the necessary changes for us to be together.

"You made Abby's day. She was bummed you guys wouldn't be able to come."

Hudson steps toward me, invading my space. "What about her mom? Was she bummed too?" he murmurs huskily.

I swallow thickly. "She's an adult and understands what happens on vacation stays on vacation." But as the words come out, even I know it's a lie—one I need to turn into the truth if I have any chance of getting over the man who has stolen my heart.

"I don't agree with that," Hudson says, taking my chin between his fingers and lifting my face up to look at him. "You came to my home, met my friends, slept in my bed. You made breakfast in my kitchen after I spent the night making you come several times. This is more than a vacation fling, and you know it." He presses his lips to mine, and I sigh into him, drinking him in like a dehydrated plant desperate for water.

"I've missed you, baby," he whispers against my lips, making my body thrum in need. "Have you missed me?"

"It doesn't matter. Nothing's changed."

His forehead drops softly against my own. "It does matter. It matters a helluva lot."

Our reunion is cut off by the sound of a throat clearing, and when I turn around, I find my dad standing on the porch with his arms crossed over his chest, glaring daggers at the man who's still holding me in his arms.

"Hey, Dad," I say, stepping out of Hudson's hold. "Hudson, this is my dad, Charles. Dad, this is Hudson, Lucas and Presley's dad."

"Seems like he's a bit more than *just* a dad," he bites out, no doubt recalling the couple of conversations we've had since we've returned from Hilton Head, and every time I've chalked it up to a couple of single parents hanging out with our kids who became fast friends. When I told them we were flying to New York, my parents gave me a curious look but thankfully didn't ask questions when I explained we were invited to see the city. When I sent the invitation, at Abby's request, I figured if Hudson actually RSVP'd, I could give them a more detailed version before he arrived. Only he said he couldn't go...

"It's nice to meet you, sir," Hudson says, shaking my dad's hand. "And you're right, despite the fact your daughter wants to downplay what's happening between us, I am more than just Presley and Lucas's dad. I'm in love with your daughter."

Dad's eyes go wide, and at the same time, I gasp in shock at Hudson's bluntness.

"Is that right?" Dad says. "Then it's a good thing you're here so we can get to know each other."

"You know who he is," I mutter. "You watch football."

"True, I know who the football player is, but that doesn't tell me anything about the man behind the helmet." He steps over to Hudson and pats his back. "So, Hudson, let's start with what your intentions are with my daughter. I hear that you love her, but what I want to know is, what does that mean?"

"Oh God," I groan, wondering how the hell Hudson thinks he's going to talk his way out of this one since we don't even know where we stand.

"What it means," Hudson begins, his eyes locking on mine, "is, while we have a few bumps in the road to get over, I have every intention of making Sawyer mine in every way that matters."

At his admission, butterflies swarm in my chest, wishing it were that simple but knowing it's not.

"That's a good start," Dad says, his tone ringing with approval. "Let's go out back. I'm sure my wife will be excited to meet you. Like me, she had no idea Sawyer left on vacation and came back in love."

And. Kill. Me. Now.

As we walk through the house to the back, I give Hudson the ten-cent tour. When we walk outside, my sister locks eyes with me, then her gaze goes to Hudson, and she smirks.

Fuck. My dad has nothing on my sister.

"Hudson." She opens her arms and gives him an overzealous hug. "So nice to see you again. Glad you and your kids could make it."

"Thanks," he says, hugging her back like they're family. "Thought I would surprise Sawyer." He glances at me and winks. "I think it worked."

Lisa cracks up laughing. "The only thing my sister hates more than football is being surprised."

This time, it's Hudson's turn to laugh.

"Did you have a good rest of your vacation?" Lisa asks, sitting back down and pulling out a chair at the table she's sitting at for Hudson.

"I did. Not as much fun once Sawyer and Abby left, but it was nice. Relaxing."

"Left from where?" my mom asks, walking over and joining in on the conversation. "And who might you be? Wait, don't tell me. You must be the father of those adorable kids who ran through here with my granddaughter."

"That would be me." He takes her hand and kisses the top of it. "It's nice to meet you, ma'am. Hudson Matthews."

"Oh, please. Call me Lori."

"The man declared his love for our daughter in the driveway, Lor," Dad announces. "At this rate, he'll be calling you Mom soon."

I close my eyes and beg for the ground to swallow me up while my mom gasps in shock. "Oh my. Sawyer never..."

"Mentioned anything," Hudson finishes. "I can see that. She's a little in denial right now, but I'm working on getting her caught up to speed."

Lisa snorts out a laugh, and my mom giggles. Freaking giggles. Of course he's here not even two minutes, and he's already gained my father's respect and has my mom and sister eating out of his hand.

"Mommy, can we go in the bounce house?" Abby asks, running over excitedly. "Uncle Scott said he'll watch us."

"Sure, just be careful."

"I will!"

She runs back to where the bounce house is set up and jumps in, with Presley and Lucas following.

Luckily, the guests start to arrive before my family can pry us with any more questions.

We spend the morning watching the kids play in the bounce house, then switch to the slip-and-slide. Hudson shocks me when he throws on some board shorts and joins them, flying down the water trap and sailing into the pool at the end. The kids all gang up on him, jumping into the pool and splashing him.

"He's quite the catch," Mom whispers into my ear. "Good career, doting father, doesn't have a fear of commitment..."

"A thousand miles away, an NFL player who travels half the year..."

"Sawyer, get over here and save me!" Hudson yells in a playful tone.

When I shake my head, he nods slowly, a glint in his eye, telling me if I don't do as he says, he'll ensure I do. Not wanting him to carry me over his shoulder in front of half the parents in this town—including my own—I peel off my tank top, leaving me in only my bikini top and cutoffs, and walk over to where Hudson is.

"Happy?" I ask, popping my hip out.

"Not yet..." He lifts up and grabs me by my hips, pulling me down with him into the mini pool. The water splashes around us, and the kids laugh as I'm soaked from head to toe. Once I'm sideways in his lap, he pushes the wet strands of my hair from out of my eyes, a boyish grin lighting up his face. "There," he says. "Now, I'm happy."

"I'm so going to get you back for this," I whisper. Our eyes lock, and for a second, I forget we're surrounded by dozens of people and kids. My tongue darts out, wetting my lips, and Hudson's gaze falls to my mouth. We both lean in at the same time for a kiss when my daughter's voice rings out, shaking us out of our trance. I climb out of his lap and stand, glancing around for my daughter while avoiding looking at anyone else in fear they were just watching us. People in small towns talk, and by the way they've been eyeing Hudson, I imagine they know exactly who he is. The last thing I need is to give them something to gossip about.

"Mommy, come jump with me!" Abby yells.

"Dad! Come jump too," Lucas adds.

"HEY, MAN, YOU'RE HUDSON MATTHEWS...THE QB FOR THE

Bluebirds, right?" Tim, the father of one of Abby's friends, and the husband of Deann, a friend of mine from high school, asks while we're all eating lunch. My mom and I made platters of sandwiches and side dishes to keep it simple so my dad wouldn't have to spend the day at the grill.

Hudson's sitting next to me, eating one-handed with his other hand on my thigh, massaging circles into my flesh. The second Tim speaks to him, his hand comes to a halt, squeezing me gently. His back stiffens, and a fake smile tips at the corners of his lips. "I am," he says, not giving him anything else. I kind of expected more people to know about him since our photos of us from my trip to New York are all over the internet, but most people who live here don't care about what's being posted on gossip sites. They're too busy trying to make a living. But that doesn't stop the men from watching football...

"I'm a huge fan," Tim says. "Born and raised in New York. Moved here for college, but the Bluebirds will always be my team. Glad you decided to renew your contract."

"Thanks for your support," Hudson says robotically.

"Think you'll bring home another ring?" Tim asks.

"That's the plan." Hudson takes a bite of his macaroni salad, relaxing slightly when it seems like the conversation is over.

"So, you play football in New York?" Deann, ever the nosy one, asks, not allowing the subject to drop. "How did you guys meet?"

"Our kids hit it off at the resort camp we were staying at earlier this summer," I explain quickly.

"That's so nice. Long flight to come to a birthday party," Stacy, Deann's sister, quips with a knowing smirk.

"Who's ready for presents?" I call out to nobody, trying to change the subject.

Hudson's hand tightens on my thigh, and I take a deep breath, having no idea how to handle any of this. It's one thing for my family to be aware we have something going on, but it's another for everyone to know. The last guy I allowed myself to get close to, chose his career over his daughter and me. The looks of pity I received for months after it got out was nearly enough to drive me out of town. I can't imagine the looks I'd get if they knew about Hudson and me, only to learn he walked away as well...And he will walk away. He doesn't have a choice.

"Sawyer," Mom chides. "Presents are last. We haven't even had cake yet. Besides, Abby is still eating her lunch with her friends."

I sigh. "I'm going to go grab another drink. Hudson, want one?"

"Sure," he says around his food, loosening his grip on me.

"Why don't you come pick it out? I'm not sure what you like."

He follows me into the house while I ignore the heat of everyone's stares on my back.

The second we're inside, Hudson corners me against the counter, his hands threading through my hair and his mouth attacking my own.

"Fuck, I've been wanting to do that since I got here," he growls when the kiss ends. "I've missed these lips so damn much." He rests his forehead against mine. "I can't do this..." He shakes his head back and forth.

"Do what?" I breathe.

"Go weeks without seeing you."

"Well, you better get used to it," I say, pushing him away

slightly. "Because regardless of what you're telling my family, we still live a thousand miles apart, and once school starts and your football season officially begins, we won't be able to hop on a plane to see each other." Tears of frustration sting my eyes, and I dart my gaze away from Hudson, hating how emotional I suddenly am. "We can't do this," I mutter. "We have to cut ties. We're only going to hurt each other if we continue like this."

"Do you still love me, Sawyer?" he asks, framing my face.

"I..."

"Don't lie to me. I want the truth."

"Yes, I love you, Hudson. I wish I didn't because then it would be easier to walk away from you, but I do. I love you so damn much."

A smile, a real one, unlike the fake one from earlier, spreads across his face just before his mouth connects with mine in a slow, passionate kiss. He lifts me onto the counter and steps between my legs, and my arms wrap around his neck, pulling him closer. Our kiss deepens, as if we're both trying to convey every emotion we feel with our mouths.

"I love you too," he murmurs against my lips, lifting me

back off the counter. "I need you. Now." My brain screams I shouldn't be doing this. I should be pushing him away, but my body tingles in response.

"Bathroom," I breathe, hooking my legs around his waist.

The second we're behind the closed door, our clothes are ripped from our bodies. Hudson spreads my legs wide, pulling me to the edge of the vanity, and enters me in one deep thrust.

I cry out, the feeling of him in me damn near sending me over the edge. He pumps in and out while peppering kisses all over my face and neck and giving my breasts special attention. His hands grip my thighs to hold on to me while he fucks me hard and fast.

"Rub that clit, baby," he murmurs, suckling on the sensitive flesh just above my collarbone.

My finger finds the sensitive nub, and in doing so, I can feel him thrusting in and out of me. The closer I get to finding my release, the harder he fucks me. Just as I'm about to come, I remember something...

"No condom," I moan as I come so hard my entire body convulses.

Hudson picks up his pace, fucking me through my orgasm, and then he pulls out, his fist wrapping around his hard length and stroking it a couple of times before ropes of cum hit my stomach and thighs.

"Holy shit," he breathes, dropping his forehead against mine. "We're going to have to figure something out because I need you, Sawyer. I can't go weeks, let alone days without you."

His words, utterly unexpected at this moment, cause my throat to tighten with emotion. I nod, agreeing with him because I feel the same way, but I don't say anything because, despite how we feel, I don't have an answer to our problem.

Fourteen

Hudson

"THIS IS ALL YOUR LAND?" I ASK IN AWE FROM THE PASSENGER seat of the side-by-side. The kids are sitting in the back, enjoying the off-road ride, while Sawyer shows me around her property. The birthday party ended about an hour ago, and when she asked if I'd like a tour of the property, I couldn't pass it up. It's beautiful out here, and I can see why she loves it.

"Yep," she says. "Over three hundred acres of farmland. My family deals in livestock...Cattle, dairy, chickens. We also have a large greenhouse with fruits and vegetables, and my mom breeds and trains horses as well."

"I have a lot of horses," Abby chimes in.

"I wanna ride a horse," Presley adds.

"I can show you," Abby tells her, pride evident in her voice. "I'm really good. Right, Mommy? I have three ribbons."

"Yes, you are," Sawyer says.

She's driving toward what looks like the end of her property when I notice a for sale sign at the front of the road. "It's for sale?"

"Yeah. My dad had set that property aside in case we wanted to build a house and live on the farm, but my brother had other plans, and my sister travels too much to put down roots in this small town. He doesn't need all this land, and with big businesses taking over, the demand has reduced. With technology, they can produce higher quantities at a lower price...even if the quality isn't as good. We sell to a lot of the businesses in town and some of the surrounding area, but it's been a struggle. Dad's going to sell this property and use the money to buy some much-needed equipment for the farm, to try to get caught up with the times."

As she drives us around, stopping at the cows, chickens,

and horses, I find myself asking a million questions, curious about everything. It's a completely different type of lifestyle than living in the city, and I never pictured myself living on a farm, but as she explains everything, my mind is swirling with thoughts and ideas. Ones I'm not quite ready to voice yet...

When we get back to her parents' place, where she lives with Abby, the kids ask if they can go riding, which gives me the perfect opening I need.

"Do you have to get going soon?" Sawyer asks, the look in her eyes telling me she's dreading me leaving as much as I am.

"We have a hotel booked for tonight and tomorrow at the bed and breakfast in town. We're not leaving until Monday."

"Really?" she asks in shock. "What about training camp?"

"I took a couple of days off." I shrug nonchalantly even though I got hell over it. Taking days off during training camp is frowned upon, and I've never done it before, but I couldn't find it in me to care. Coming here, being with Sawyer, and spending Abby's birthday with her was more important.

"How was the tour?" Charlie asks, walking over, now dressed in a pair of Wranglers, a button-down flannel shirt, and cowboy boots.

"Good," I tell him. "Sawyer was about to take the kids to ride the horses. But I was thinking I could join you if that's okay."

Sawyer eyes me curiously, but before she can ask why, her dad nods and says, "Sure, I'm about to go do my afternoon chores."

"Sounds good." I glance down at my flip-flops. "Any chance you have a pair of boots you can lend me?"

Sawyer laughs. "I can give you a pair of mud boots." She grabs the front of my shirt and drags me toward the barn and into the tackle room. "Why are you trying to hang out with my dad?" she asks, shoving a pair of black rubbers boots at me.

"I just want to learn about the place." And see if the thoughts whirling in my head can possibly be brought to fruition.

She hits me with a *you're full of shit* look but doesn't push. "Fine. Have fun, cityboy."

"YOU'RE SERIOUSLY NOT GOING TO TELL ME?" SAWYER WHINES.

The kids are inside watching a movie, her mom spoiling them with popcorn and candy, while Sawyer and I are sitting on the porch swing with my arms wrapped around her, her head pressed up against my chest, and her body flush against mine. It's dark outside, the only light coming in from the stars shining bright in the sky.

"No, it's between your dad and me," I tell her, dipping my head and giving her temple a kiss. "What are we doing tomorrow? I was thinking you could show me around town."

She momentarily stiffens against me and then relaxes. "Is that what you want to do?"

"I wouldn't have asked."

"I know...It's just...It's not like New York. It's quiet...and kind of boring."

"It's where you live, and I want to know everything about you."

I close my eyes, resting my chin on the top of her head, and let the silence fill the air. It's nice being here with Sawyer, like we're back in our own little bubble. Every time I have her in my arms, a sense of serenity flows through my body that I didn't realize I was craving until her.

Eventually, the soft sound of Sawyer snoring tells me she's fallen asleep, so I pick her up and carry her up to her room. She barely stirs as I cover her with her blankets and kiss her forehead.

When I get back downstairs, the kids are all passed out as well, sprawled out across the couches like cute little starfishes.

"Why don't you stay here tonight?" Lori says, walking over next to me. "It's been a long day. No reason to lug them into the car and drive all the way into town."

"Thanks. Do you have a guest room? Or I could sleep on the couch." Though, they are currently full at the moment.

"Sawyer is a grown adult. You can sleep in there with her, and I'll get up with the kids in the morning. When you're ready, come down and join us."

I glance at her, unsure if that's the right thing to do. "If it's okay with you, I'd rather sleep in a guest room or on the couch. I think it would be disrespectful to sleep with Sawyer under your roof."

"Oh, please." She laughs. "We're country folk, but we're not that old. Go on. Get some sleep. And Hudson..." She gives me a soft smile, reminding me of Sawyer. "My husband told me about your conversation. Before you mention it to Sawyer, please make sure you're one-hundred-percent positive. I know nothing in life is guaranteed, but she was already left behind once. I'd rather her not be hurt like that a second time."

I nod in understanding, then, after kissing my kids good night, head outside to grab some clothes from my luggage. After changing into a pair of sweats and a T-shirt, I join Sawyer in bed. She's facing away from me, so I cage her into my arms. As if sensing me, she sighs against me, still asleep, and I burrow my face into her neck, falling asleep to the scent of lavender mixed with Sawyer.

"I DON'T WANNA GO," PRESLEY CRIES. "I WANNA STAY WITH ABBY and Copper." Copper is the horse my daughter has fallen in love with. She even woke up early yesterday morning to help muck his stall, feed him, and go for a ride. We spent the morning and early afternoon exploring the town. Sawyer showed us the schools, their favorite eating spots, where to get the best ice cream, and where the kids all play. When we got back after lunch, we spent the afternoon riding the horses and four-wheelers, going swimming in the pond that has a cool tree swing Lucas must've swung on and jumped off into the water a hundred times, and picking fresh fruits and vegetables to use for dinner. The kids didn't once touch or even ask for any electronics, and when it was time to go to bed, they passed out within minutes from exhaustion.

"This is so stupid," Lucas says. "Can't we just stay here? You have to go to work anyway. We can have fun here and go home when it's time for school."

The idea of leaving my kids in another state has my stomach filling with lead. It's not an option anyway, but the fact that they would even want to stay here instead of coming home with me has me feeling like a shitty dad and solidifying what I've been thinking...It's time for a change.

"You can't stay here," I tell them. "But hopefully, we can

come back soon."

"Fine." Lucas stomps outside without saying bye to anyone while Presley gives Abby and Sawyer a hug goodbye.

"Thank you for having us," I tell Sawyer, kissing her cheek.

"Thank you for coming," she says back, her words cracking at the end.

Her eyes are glassy, filled with unshed tears, and I hate that I have to leave at all. But I have responsibilities and obligations back in New York.

When we walk outside, Lucas is waiting against the side of the SUV since it's locked, and Sawyer walks over to him, bending to his level. I can't hear what she says, but he nods a couple of times, then wraps his arms around her for a hug that has my chest cracking open and my heart falling out onto the ground.

When she steps back, I notice the tears she was trying to hold in lose their battle and slide down her cheeks as she turns and walks away, sidling up next to Abby, who looks just as sad.

My eyes lock with Charles and Lori, who both nod and

smile, giving me the strength to walk away.

The ride to the airport and the flight home is long, and the kids are cranky. When we get home, they both retreat to their rooms and fall asleep early.

I pace back and forth in my room for hours, weighing the pros and cons of the decision I need to make. Around midnight, I pour myself a glass of whiskey and spend another couple of hours trying to figure out what to do. At one in the morning, I consider calling my mom for advice, but before I can, a text comes in from Sawyer. It's a picture of her in bed with a soft, sleepy smile on her face. **Miss you and the kids already.**

And just like that, with one picture, one text, my mind is made up. This woman is the one. I can feel it in every fiber of my being, and that only leaves me one choice. I send her back a text, telling her I miss her as well, and then get to work planning the next chapter of my life...of *our* life.

"MR. MATTHEWS." THE BLUEBIRD'S OWNER SHAKES MY HAND

when I walk into the meeting my agent has put together.

"Mr. Jamison, thank you for meeting with me."

We all congregate around a large rectangular table—my coach, agent, attorney, as well as a few others who have a stake in the team's future—and I repeat a similar version to what I told my agent yesterday. "I've loved every minute of my time in the NFL, and I'm so thankful for you guys taking a chance on me fifteen years ago, but I've made the decision to retire. I'm requesting to terminate the contract I recently signed."

"Is there anything we can do to change your mind?" Jamison asks, all business.

"Not unless you're planning to move the team to Tennessee."

An hour and several signed documents later, I walk out of the meeting with several pounds of weight off my shoulders.

"Dad, you're home!" Presley exclaims.

"I am. Where's your brother?"

"He's being mean." She rolls her eyes. "Joanie said to let him pout alone."

I had her keep the kids home from camp, knowing I'd be

home early and want to talk to them. "I'm going to go get him so we can talk."

Her brows furrow. "Are we in trouble?"

"No." I head upstairs and find Lucas reading again. When I knock, he doesn't say a word. "I need to talk to you and your sister."

"Why?"

"Lucas..." I warn, making it clear in my tone that regardless of how mad he is, his attitude isn't acceptable.

"Fine." He sighs, dropping his book on his bed.

Once the kids are on the couch, I sit across from them on the coffee table. "How would you feel about moving to Tennessee?"

Both of them perk up.

"Like forever?" Lucas asks.

"To live with Abby and Sawyer?" Presley asks.

"Will I have my own room?" Lucas.

"Can I share a room with Abby?" Presley.

"Wait, are you sending us away?" Lucas asks, his brows dipping in concern.

"What?" Presley gasps. "We're leaving you? I don't wanna

leave you."

"Whoa, calm down," I say with a light chuckle. "Nobody is getting sent anywhere. After spending the weekend on the farm, I think it would be a nice place to live...all of us, together on the property like where Abby's grandparents live."

Both kids nod in understanding.

"I like it there," Presley says. "Can I get a horse?"

"Yeah, me too," Lucas adds. "Can I get my own four-wheeler? Wait, is there a golf course there?"

"One step at a time," I tell them with a laugh.

"Okay, so what's the first step?" Lucas asks.

"I'm glad you asked..."

Fifteen

Sawyer

"DO YOU KNOW HOW EXPENSIVE IT IS TO LIVE IN NEW YORK?" I ask my mom, slamming my laptop closed in frustration. It's been less than a week since Hudson and his kids left, and I'm missing them like crazy. Abby has asked no less than a dozen times when she's going to see them again, and every time that I've told her I don't know, she's glared daggers my way like I'm the bad guy.

"I've only lived here," my mom says, patting my leg. "But I've heard it can be pricey."

I thought when I woke up the morning after they left

and announced that I'm planning to move to New York to be with Hudson, since I can teach anywhere, but he can only play football for the team where he lives, my parents would freak out. Instead, they both hugged me and said they're happy I've found love. I've spent the past few days researching places to live since I can't just move in with him because that would be crazy, and jobs available, since I'm going to need one to pay my bills, but I've quickly learned New York is overpriced and teachers are underpaid. I woke up Monday morning, excited and ready to let love guide me, only to be completely defeated by Friday.

"Maybe we can just keep doing the long-distance thing for a while," I say, rubbing my aching chest. "I can save up money, and once I have enough for a place, we can make the move."

Mom nods, distracted by her phone. "That sounds like a plan." She glances up at me. "Do you have Instagram?"

"Umm, yeah…"

"Can you pull it up for me, please?"

"Sure." I click on the app and hand her my phone.

After a few seconds, a familiar voice comes over my

speaker, catching Abby's attention.

"Is that Lucas?" she asks, walking over and climbing into my lap.

"It is," Mom says, turning the phone so Abby and I can both see. She presses play, and the video starts over, Lucas, Presley, and Hudson's faces appearing on the screen.

"We're here to announce," Lucas begins, a grin splayed across his face, "that our dad has decided to retire from playing football."

I gasp in shock as Presley begins to speak. "We know you'll miss him throwing the ball, but we're so excited to have our daddy at home!"

My head is spinning as Hudson smiles at both his kids before turning his attention on the camera. "It's true," he says. "I'm so thankful for the fifteen years I've been with the Bluebirds, for everything the NFL has done for me, and for all of the fans who have watched and cheered us on game after game. I've made the difficult decision to retire so I can spend more time with my kids. I know it's last minute, but I can assure you the Bluebirds have an amazing QB coming in, and I have faith they'll continue to kick ass."

"Daddy, you cursed," Presley says, making Hudson laugh.

"Sorry, sweetie." He kisses the top of her head. "Thank you to everyone who has supported me. It's been a wild ride. Go Bluebirds."

He leans forward, and the video cuts off, and I'm left in shock. He's retired. He's actually quit his job to be home with his kids. Yet nothing has changed with us because I'm still here and he's still there.

I dial his number to call and congratulate him—and also to ask why he hasn't once mentioned this every time we've spoken or texted the last few days—but his phone goes to voicemail.

"Hey, Sawyer," Dad calls out. "I'm meeting with the buyer of the property. Would you mind taking a ride with me?"

"What? You sold the property? Since when?"

"Since he made a cash offer I couldn't refuse."

"Wow, that's awesome!" I hug my dad, so happy for him and my mom. "Of course I'll go with you. Is it anyone we know? What are they planning to do with it?"

My dad chuckles. "I'll let him tell you all that."

When we arrive at the front of the road on the other side

of the property, a metallic SUV is parked and waiting for us. As I'm jumping out of the side-by-side, the vehicle doors open, and Lucas and Presley come running down the dirt road toward me.

"What are you guys doing here?" I ask in shock at seeing them.

"We're moving here!" Presley shouts in excitement, throwing her arms around my middle. "Daddy quit football, and we get to live here, and I get to go to school with Abby."

"Dad's gonna buy me a four-wheeler, and he said there's a golf course close by."

My words are stuck in my throat, confused and excited, so I do the only thing I can do. I hug them both and tell them I'm so happy they're here.

"All right, you two," my dad says. "Jump in so I can take you to Lori and Abby. There are pancakes and eggs with your names on them." He winks at me and slides back into the side-by-side, taking off with the kids.

"Surprise," Hudson says once we're alone.

"I don't understand."

"I told you I would figure it out, and I did." He leans

against the wooden post holding up the for sale sign and crosses his arms over his chest. "Your dad and I talked while I was here. I purchased the property from him at his asking price, and in exchange, he's going to teach me about farming. We'll become partners of sorts. I'm also going to be building a house out here."

"You're...you're going to be my neighbor?" This is all so crazy. One minute, he's living in New York, preparing for the upcoming football season, and the next, he's standing in front of me telling me he's...moving here?

Hudson pushes off the post and bridges the gap between us, dropping onto his knee. "I'm actually hoping we'll be more than that." He opens a small black box, and a shiny ring sparkles in the sunlight. My hands go to my mouth, and his eyes lock with mine.

"I want to build that home with you," he says, a small smile curling on his lips. "I want to create a home and a life with you, with our kids. What do you say, Sawyer? Will you marry me?"

There are probably a million reasons I should say no, and tell him this is too soon, too fast. We've only known each other for a short time. But as he stares up at me with love in his eyes, there's only one answer that feels right.

"Yes," I tell him. "Yes, I'll marry you."

Epilogue

Sawyer

FIVE YEARS LATER

HUDSON'S STRONG HAND GLIDES ALONG MY HIP AND ACROSS my stomach, stopping just above my belly button. He gently strokes my flesh while his warm lips pepper kisses across the back of my shoulder. My eyes flutter open as I inhale the fresh scent of the salt water. It's still early, the yellowish-orange sun barely peeking out from behind the ocean.

"Spread your thighs, baby," he murmurs huskily, his voice laced with a mixture of sleep and need.

I set my foot on top of his thigh, giving him access, and

he pushes into me from behind, filling me completely. His hand ascends to my breast, stroking my pebbled nipple and then pinching it hard. I moan in pleasure, loving how my husband always knows exactly what to do to make me feel good.

As he slowly slides in and out of me, making love to me, his mouth moves to the sensitive spot on my neck, between my ear and shoulder, suckling on my flesh. His fingers release my nipple, and he takes my hand in his, bringing it back up to my breast.

"Play with your nipples," he demands tenderly, letting go and finding the sensitive nub between my legs. He massages my clit with gentle strokes while he continues to push in and out of me, his dick hitting me in all the right places. My orgasm is a slow build, little by little, until I'm teetering on the precipice. With a final caress, I fall into the abyss, taking Hudson with me.

He pulls out and rolls over on top of me, his arms caging me in. He dips his head and takes my bottom lip into his mouth, then my top, before he connects his mouth to mine in a passionate kiss. "Happy anniversary," he whispers against my mouth. "I can't believe it took us this long to get back here."

Here being on the island where we met. It's been a crazy five years between getting engaged, planning a wedding, building a house, and helping my dad modernize and expand the farm, all while raising three kids and me teaching full-time.

"It was worth the wait." I lift up and peck his lips. "I can't believe you bought this place." As an anniversary gift, Hudson surprised me by buying us a beach house on the island with its own private beach.

"It's the only way I could ensure I'd be able to sleep naked under the stars with you." He glides his body downward, stopping at my belly and giving it a soft kiss. As his lips caress my flesh, the baby releases a strong kick, making us laugh. "I think that's his way of saying it's getting crowded in there."

"Only a few more months, little guy," he says to the baby, kissing my belly again.

My stomach rumbles in hunger, and Hudson glances up at me.

"I think he's hungry." I giggle.

"Oh, is he? And what is he hungry for?"

"Hmm..." I tap my finger to my chin and look up at the sky in thought. "Chocolate chip pancakes... with peanut butter on them, and bacon... mmm." I groan, suddenly starved. "Watermelon, too," I add, my mouth watering.

Hudson chuckles and sits up, grabbing our clothes. "Your wish is my command."

Once we're dressed, we head back up to the house. It's quiet, the kids still asleep, along with my parents, who I convinced to join us on our trip. It's their first time at the beach, and they're already talking about where else they want to travel.

As Hudson sets about making breakfast while I sit on the stool and watch, the kids, one by one, wake up. Abby comes out first, going straight to the kitchen. She walks around Hudson, stopping only long enough to kiss him on the cheek and mutter, "Morning, Dad," sleepily before she takes some chocolate chips from the bag and joins me on the stool next to mine, resting her head on my shoulder and popping them into her mouth.

The first time she called Hudson "Dad," he glanced at me with glassy eyes in shock and awe. We'd been together for a few months at that point, and it came out by mistake, most likely because Lucas and Presley called him Dad all the time. She didn't mention it, and he didn't make a big deal out of it.

I honestly didn't even think she realized she did it. Until later that night, while we were putting the girls to bed, Hudson kissed them both and Presley said, "'Night, Daddy!"

Abby glanced at Hudson like she wanted to say something.

"Hey, you okay?" Hudson asked, sitting on the edge of her bed.

She nodded slowly, then looked at me. "Mommy, where's my daddy?"

I stilled in my place, unsure what to say. After a few seconds, I went for the truth. "I'm not sure, sweetie."

"Why doesn't he want to be my daddy?" she asked, breaking my heart.

Again, I told her the only truth I could give her. "Not everyone is meant to be a mom and a dad."

Her nose scrunched up, and I knew she didn't get it. But before I could try to explain, Hudson spoke up.

"Every baby is a gift," he explained. "Some gifts we keep for ourselves, and other gifts we give to others. Like on your birthday, when everyone brings you gifts."

"So, I'm a gift?" she asked, her little brow furrowing.

"The best gift your mom and I have ever been given," he told her, kissing her forehead.

"Am I a gift, too?" Presley asked.

"A very special gift," Hudson said to her, making her beam.

"Can you be my daddy?" Abby asked hesitantly.

"Absolutely," he told her without a second thought.

From that day forward, Abby called him Dad, and a few weeks later, Lucas and Presley started calling me Mom. There wasn't a discussion that took place. It just happened naturally.

While the pancakes and bacon are cooking, Hudson slices up some watermelon and strawberries and sets them in a bowl in front of me so I can snack while he makes breakfast.

A few minutes later, Presley joins us. She does the same thing her sister did, kissing her dad on the cheek, muttering good morning, and stealing some chocolate chips. This time he's ready, though, and the second her hand goes into the bag, he swats it with the spatula playfully.

"Hey," she grumbles, glaring at him.

"Breakfast will be ready soon," he tells her, going back to cooking.

She looks like she's going to walk away, but right before she does, she turns around quickly and swipes a handful, running away while cackling. Hudson tries to grab her, but she gets away.

"I'm going to take a shower!" she calls out. "Let me know when breakfast is ready."

"Morning," Lucas says, stumbling in half-asleep. "Smells good. I'm starved." He reaches for his phone that's sitting on the counter since they're not allowed to take them to bed with them, and plops on the stool on the other side of me, most likely texting his new girlfriend good morning.

A little while later, my parents come out, wishing everyone a good morning and letting us know they're going to go for a walk and to have breakfast at the café up the beach.

As Hudson is setting the food on the table, Presley joins

us, freshly showered and in her bathing suit and cover-up. Lucas grabs everyone a drink while I set the table.

As I watch everyone dig into their food, I can't help the smile that spreads across my face. My entire world is right here, under one roof.

I pull my phone out of my pocket and turn slightly, snapping a quick picture.

"I'd stop taking selfies with the food and eat it before these vultures inhale it first," Hudson warns.

"I wasn't taking a picture of the food," I say with a laugh, pulling the photo up. When I show it to him, he smiles a soft smile and nods, no doubt seeing what I see.

It's a picture of our family.

Of our life.

Of what love looks like.

About the Author

Reading is like breathing in, writing is like breathing out. – Pam Allyn

Nikki Ash resides in South Florida where she is an English teacher by day and a writer by night. When she's not writing, you can find her with a book in her hand. From the Boxcar Children, to Wuthering Heights, to the latest single parent romance, she has lived and breathed every type of book. While reading and writing are her passions, her two children are her entire world. You can probably find them at a Disney park before you would find them at home on the weekends!